JUNKYARD
WAR

Books by Faith Hunter

The Jane Yellowrock Series
SKINWALKER

BLOOD CROSS

MERCY BLADE

RAVEN CURSED

DEATH'S RIVAL

BLOOD TRADE

BLACK ARTS

BROKEN SOUL

DARK HEIR

SHADOW RIGHTS

COLD REIGN

THE JANE YELLOWROCK WORLD COMPANION

DARK QUEEN

SHATTERED BONDS

TRUE DEAD

FINAL HEIR

Compilations
BLOOD IN HER VEINS

OF CLAWS AND FANGS

continued...

JUNKYARD
WAR

novella 3

FAITH HUNTER

LORE
SEEKERS
PRESS

JUNKYARD WAR
ISBN 978-1-62268-178-5
Copyright © 2022 Faith Hunter

Also available in e-book form: ISBN 978-1-62268-177-8

Cover illustration by Rebecca Frank, Bewitching Book Covers.

Printed in the United States of America on acid-free paper.

Lore Seekers Press is an imprint of Bella Rosa Books.
Lore Seekers Press and logo are trademarks of Bella Rosa Books.

10   9   8   7   6   5   4   3   2   1

Acknowledgments

No book is written in a vacuum. This novella, and the entire Junkyard Cats series, has been dependent on several people.

Editor Steve Feldberg at Audible for all the wonderful suggestions and insights for the Audible Original. Every care has been taken to deviate not at all.

Agent Lucienne Diver with The Knight Agency for acquiring an Audible Original for the Junkyard Cats series.

Cover design by Rebecca Frank of Bewitching Book Covers. Love it!

Robert Martin, physicist and theoretical physicist-adventurer. The creator of the science behind the WIMP engines and the EntNu communications system in the Junkyard Universe.

Bonnie Smietanowska, physicist.

Mud Mumudes for all things plant-ish and genetic-y.

Brenda Rezk for breaking down genetic stuff I couldn't understand.

William Joseph Roberts aka Hillbilly for biker club info.

Teri Lee Akar editor extraordinaire.

Let's Talk Promotions for running PR.

And to Lore Seekers Press for the e-book and print editions, thank you.

JUNKYARD
WAR

"Reconnoiter via feral cats. This is a first," Mateo said into my helmet's communications system. There might have been humor in the words. Hard to tell through his metallic larynx.

"Cats approaching outer perimeter. And they ain't feral, CO Sugah," Jolene said. "The pride done named themselves *Felis catus destructus*."

I looked up from the small screen I had opened in my helmet's vid display. "The pride cats understand Latin?"

"Prolly," the AI back at the USSS *SunStar* said, in the Southern accent she chose for herself. "But Tuffs just kinda asked me for help and we came up with it together."

I didn't know which was the worse possibility, the pride cats speaking Latin or the not-supposed-to-be-sentient-but-was AI talking with the not-supposed-to-be-sentient-but-were cats. "Fine. Whatever."

Mateo snorted. It was a grating sound I interpreted as laughter. There wasn't much left of one side of his head, and part of his throat had been so damaged by swarming PRC nanobots that my med-bay had implanted an artificial one I'd bartered for at an illegal swap meet. Medical supplies had been hard to come by back then, and still were. Mateo also didn't have all his limbs, which I hadn't been able to fix, and lived most of his life in the neural-net-controlled warbot.

I could practically feel him looming above me, seven and a half meters of legs, torso, and head with a meter of horizontal silk-plaz view screen. With his dynamic environmental camouflage off, the warbot suit looked like the love child of a deadly spider and a kid's toy, and if this recce went sideways, Mateo's suit and his battle tank, situated half a click away, might be the only reason we got out of here.

"The cats got through the outer perimeter, y'all," Jolene said. "We got visuals from both of the cameras."

Even with night-vision goggles, it was hard to tell much. The cams had been mounted on the chests of the cats' tactical harnesses to make it harder for sensors to spot them, and they were emplaced to give us a good angle and line of sight, but there was only so much we could see with the cams at fifteen centimeters off the ground. Spy and her mate, Maul, were currently running—that crouched-predator sprint-stop-sprint, of cats—through autumn-dry prairie grasses, giving us no actual view of the target: a heavily fortified and armed World War III bunker.

I fidgeted as the cats approached what had looked like a small overgrown hill in the drone flyovers we had done. It had taken us weeks to get to the stage of in-person reconnoiter and, as patient as I had been, now I was jumpy, jittery, and my armor readouts showed it. I tried to relax. Wasn't helping. Where was the bloody damn bunker? The cats should be right on top of it.

In the last weeks we had created cat-sized tac harnesses with comms systems, destroyed the nanobots infesting the Simba battle tank, checked out its systems, retrofitted hardware, added new weapons, and tied the crashed spaceship's EntNu comms system to the tank. EntNu was based on the practical application of the science of entwined neutrinos and gave us instantaneous communication with Jolene back at the junkyard. All that, just so we could verify that the bunker had been taken over by our enemy, the MSA's Clarisse Warhammer, and maybe get a look inside.

Amos and Mateo had done most of the preparatory muscle work. Jolene had spent the time collecting intel on the motorcycle clubs, while Cupcake (and sometimes I) talked to intermediaries and put together the upcoming negotiations. There was a long list of potential trade items to cement the safety and cooperation of the participants— the leaders of the most successful biker clubs in what was left of the US. My plans were fluid, my goals even more so, and what I discovered from this current recce would change what I negotiated for at the parley.

Not that the biker club VIPs knew everything about the upcoming meeting. They didn't even know who was invited. The Outlaw Militia Warriors and the Hells Angels thought they were just gathering to divide up territory and discuss an ordinary war of guns in a battle against the MS Angels. They didn't know about the prisoner we wanted to rescue or what Clarisse Warhammer really was.

The MSA was what was left after the West Coast portion of the Hells Angels biker club had been usurped by the old MS-13—the Mara Salvatrucha gang. The merged criminal enterprise was bent on taking over the entire country. Warhammer was now the driving force of that move, quickly rising to the top of her own ultra-violent gang while invading the other clubs' territories.

I couldn't stop the MSA's expansion or Warhammer alone.

I'd seen Pops have these conversations with powerful men during the war—dialogues of half-truths, allusions, and insinuations to convince others to meet and talk without giving away secrets or killing each other, all while dangling the promise of monetary and territorial benefits. It had been boring when I was twelve, just watching and listening. It was *bloody damn freaking* boring when I had to do it myself. I was not cut out for politics.

One of the things we might offer the VIPs, to assure that the negotiations were successful and a treaty I liked was reached, was info on the *inside* of the bunker where Clarisse Warhammer had her nest. Warhammer, who wanted more slaves and territory, was a nanobot-modified, mutated queen who could enthrall and enslave humans. And we believed she had a prisoner in her nest, one we would need to exfil before we destroyed it.

Bad thing! Back!

Spy's fear-laden vision-smell suddenly shocked through me. Adrenaline spiked and hardened my suit armor in reaction.

A soft verbal "*Orrrowmerow siss*" followed, which in cat-speak meant *There is a bad problem and danger.* The camera mounted on her battle harness showed me what had shaken her. Two centimeters from her paw, something was sticking out of the ground. Metallic.

"Mateo?"

"Land mine. They step on it, they're goners."

I sent the image of an explosion to Spy through our newly established mental contact, and added the thought, *Stalk slow. Watch for bad things.* "Be careful," I added aloud, so Maul would hear too, on the harness's comms system.

"Mrow. Siss," Spy hissed into the small mic near the camera. *Invaders. Dangerous.* She added a soft growl, a sound I had learned meant *hunt and kill.*

Spy looked at her mate, Maul, his scars caught on her low-light camera, bright and hairless against his black fur.

Maul had chosen the name himself, after fighting his way to the top of the male mating cats. Maul, as in "he mauled and killed all the cat contenders with testicles."

He was Spy's weapon of choice, an enforcer like Jagger, my . . . whatever he was. Maul operated under the orders of the Guardian Cat queen, Tuffs, and also at the whim of Spy—his mate and Tuffs's heir.

Maul placed his head against Spy's, communicating through the spooky weird ESP crap that was the result of Tuffs being infested with my nanobots early on at the junkyard. They separated and continued on, their progress slowed, grasses passing beside them as they moved. Maul crossed a gravel two-rut road overgrown with saplings. The small trees showed signs of being driven over, though not often enough to kill them.

On my helmet screen, Jolene began generating a map of the grounds, with defenses noted in red.

Moments later, we saw dual vids of triangular reinforced concrete to either side of massive metal doors, all with dynamic enviro camo that made them look, on first glance, like boulders and dead grass.

The main entrance to the bunker was near the intersection of old I-77 and I-81, near Fort Chiswell. It had been locked up and left empty by the military at the end of the war, per orders of the Bug aliens. Except for the faint signs of traffic, visible only from up close, I wouldn't have known it was in use.

I didn't have to tell Spy what to do. She and Maul

skirted the doors and began quartering the hillock the bunker had been built into, looking for hidden or disguised entrances, noting defenses and, most important, searching for ventilation shafts. The two cats and I had studied hours of video showing the various kinds of air shafts, hidden back doors, weapons emplacements, and man-made openings used by the military so the cats could spot them without constant direction from me.

Thankfully for my temper, they found an air shaft twenty minutes later, and then four others, sticking their heads through the grates into each, evaluating their size and the smells and sensation of air moving through. The map on my face shield depicting the hillock of the buried fort grew, becoming more detailed.

The cats picked a promising duct with a rusted hole in one corner of the covering—no airflow, a flat place to work from, and an autumn-dry tree nearby to provide cover. Through the hole, the cams revealed a slanted shaft disappearing into the dark.

Maul scratched open a small pocket on Spy's vest and pulled out a rope with loops on each end. As if the cats fully understood the physics of belaying ropes—which they might, because that had been covered in the videos, too—Spy stuck her head through a loop and trotted around the small tree, pulling it taut, then moving under and over the rope itself several times, effectively making a freaking knot. Maul did the same with his. It wasn't as good as rappelling gear, but since the cats hadn't evolved fingers, the strap around the head was the best we could do.

Spy studied the inclined air shaft, breathing in the scents. *"Mehshh,"* she said softly. It was the word for *rats*. On her camera, I spotted rat droppings along both sides of the shaft.

I gave her a mental nudge and she let me in. Vertigo sent nausea through my system. I couldn't stay in her mind for long, hence the tac harnesses and comms gear. The shaft on the other side of the damaged grate was maybe 80-by-80 centimeters, and it went down at a barely manageable thirty-five-to-forty degree angle of descent. Spy crawled through the rusted hole and stopped, crouching. Her harness camera, already adjusted to night light, indicated a faint reddish glow just ahead. It was a WWIII era security camera with a tiny red light indicating it was still active. It wasn't a multi-spectrum device, and looked like a bottom-of-the-line cheapie, which made sense for an air duct.

Body in a tight ball, her paws out in front to slow any inadvertent slip, Spy moved toward the cam. Bracing her feet, she humped up to it and around to its back, where she turned and pressed her tac harness to the camera casing. I heard a faint click as the magnetized infiltrator bug attached itself to the camera's metal housing. We had practiced this maneuver, and it went off without a hitch.

Two minutes later, Jolene said, "I'm in. Deactivated security cam. Digging my way through the camera node to locate the central security system."

I chuckled and sent Spy an *atta girl* through our mental link.

Spy slid-skidded-walked down the angled shaft, her claws clicking on the metal. Spiderwebs and a nest of leaves and twigs appeared to the side in an uneven portion of the metal duct. Spy stopped, sniffed, and said, *"Mehshh."* There was a thick trail of rat droppings along both sides of the duct but no fresh scent, so I assumed the rat nest was abandoned.

Beyond it was a fan in a cowling that narrowed the shaft considerably, the fan blades unmoving. She stepped over and through it, passing a large rat skeleton tangled in the blades—probably the reason why the ventilation fan no longer turned.

A little further on, a narrow secondary shaft opened, and smells came up the passage to Spy, some of which I recognized through our mental connection—human sweat, sex, and blood. There was the smell of cooking food and the reek of a human toilet. And beneath it all was the stink of Warhammer's nanobots.

Spy said, *"Mrow. Siss."* Invaders. Dangerous. *"Kah,"* she breathed. *Enemy queen*.

Our intel had been good. Our recon crew had just confirmed the presence of Clarisse Warhammer in this bunker, somewhere. A spike of relief speared through me, trailed closely by a barb of worry. Warhammer had already attacked me and mine once. To protect us, I would have to kill the only other nanobot mutated queen I knew of, one way or another.

Spy continued along the larger tunnel, digging in her claws as it steepened or flattened and other adjacent shafts moved off into the dark. Four times she spotted cameras ahead, and Jolene turned them off. Disabling all the cameras was a key part of our strategy for the coming war. This recon was the first real indication that we might succeed.

For my small group, this would be a dual-purpose war —a war to rescue Captain Evelyn Raymond, Mateo's number one on the starship that had crashed on the back of the junkyard property; and a war of vengeance for the death of Harlan (my best friend) at the hands of Clarisse, who was holding Evelyn prisoner. Tears still prickled beneath my eyelids each time I remembered Harlan—dead, tortured, being eaten by bicolor ants, delivered to me in back of a hunk of scrap metal. And if the severed finger she had sent to me was an indication, Warhammer was now brutalizing Evelyn as well.

Warhammer had to be stopped. I would stop her.

My armor informed me that I was breathing too fast and my heart rate and blood pressure had spiked. It asked if I wanted liquids, nutrients and stimulants, or hardening and recoil adjustments. "No. I'm good," I said, forcing my breathing to smooth. "Jolene. Any update on spotting more entrances?"

"Four camouflaged entrances noted in RVAC remote flyovers, Shining Sugah. All are behind blast doors. Three appear to have been used recently. There are six air shafts, most not suitable for human use, though with cat infiltration that makes a total of ten potential entrances. Multiple entrenched and camouflaged armaments have been catalogued, but none appear to have been activated since the original abandonment, and all are overgrown with vegetation."

"Any luck seeing heat signatures, or anything that would tell us how many thralls are in there?"

"Negative, Darlin'."

This recce would determine everything. The more humans there were inside, the more help we would need to accomplish our objectives, and the more likely there would be an internal war between the biker clubs after the battle here, to take the spoils. And the more likely that we would be spotted by the military sensors and corporate satellite systems.

The coming operation to rescue Evelyn Raymond and kill Warhammer had FUBAR written all over it.

Spy reached the bottom of the shaft where its trajectory flattened out for about two meters. The shaft ended and there was a grate over the opening. Spy would have been stymied at that point, but there were teeth marks on the metal. The rats, which sometimes reached more than ten kilos, had gnawed open a hole. Through steel.

Bloody hell.

I sent a warning to Spy to remember to watch out for rats bigger than she was, and that had steel-gnawing teeth. *Bloody mutated rats.* Spy sent me an emotion that felt unimpressed and bored. In my screen, Maul dove into the shaft, following his mate. His camera showed him running-sliding down the shaft, through and past all the things that had slowed Spy, and up to her.

They bopped noses, slipped the ropes off their heads, having not actually needed them, and crawled through the rathole. Their cameras auto-adjusted to a much dimmer light. The room had large steel tanks, tables, and bins, and to Spy's nose smelled of ancient rotten fruit, old rat droppings, and piss, but there was no fresh scent of anything.

"I've seen something like this before," Mateo said. "Those are fermentation tanks for wine or beer. This was more than a war bunker."

"CO Sugah, this mighta been one of them bunkers set aside for what you might call the last resort," Jolene said, then added, "A habitation for the politicians who would rebuild the world after Armageddon. After the rest of y'all died a horrible death."

"Which would mean Warhammer has enough supplies to last years," I said.

"And a lot more weapons than we anticipated," Mateo said. "And a lot more square footage down there. The cats' GPS shows a significant increase in depth."

On the screens, I watched as the cats scouted the fermentation room. It was big, maybe fifteen by twenty meters, and abandoned rats' nests were everywhere. There were small bones of prey here and there that could have been cat or dog, hunted outside and dragged in.

"Be careful," I thought at Spy. She ignored me.

The cats followed a well-traveled rat path of droppings through a chewed hole into the next room, and wove a path into a hallway with a stairwell. Here, the scent of rat piss was strong, and fresh droppings were everywhere.

"Mehshh," Spy said again. She didn't like this place and wanted to move on, but there were doors at the next landing up, and I sent her the request to position so I could read the words on the doors. Grain Storage 24 was stenciled on one. MREs 5 was on another. All food perfect for rats. The rodents had moved from the fermentation room where they had to bring in outside kills, and had set up living quarters where there was likely enough food to last years.

A rustling sounded and Spy looked up. She met the glossy brown eyes of a monster rat. And then more pairs. And more. The rats moved forward a single step. Then another. In unison, like a marching band. Or soldiers. Or puppets.

"Mrow. Siss," she said into her small mic. *Invaders. Dangerous.* *"Orrrowmerow,"* she added. *There is a bad problem.*

"Get out," I whispered into the mic and into Spy's head. "Run."

The cats raced away, along the corridor and through another rathole. The rats didn't follow, and I pretended not to know that Spy—who had been unconcerned and blasé only moments before—was seriously freaked by steel-eating, lockstep-marching rats. I was freaked too, and nauseated from our mental contact. I pulled back a bit, following their travel on the cam feed on my screen. They ran down hallways, along plumbing pipes, through holes. I was lost when they stopped, quivering, side by side, touching all along their bodies. They seemingly conferred.

I swallowed down nausea. Oversized, mutated rats, walking like soldiers in parade formation. *Mind controlled.* What if the rats had been transitioned the way the junkyard cats had? With a rat queen? That would suck.

"You got the layout?" I asked Jolene, focusing on the floor plan she was constructing from the cat cameras' views and coordinates.

"The cats' trackers and cameras are providin' a floor plan of hallways and ratholes," she said, "but we need more information about rooms and their designations."

I returned my thoughts to Spy and sent her Jolene's instructions through our mental link. I got back a series of impressions before the cats separated, seeming calmer. They stepped out, their gaits smoother.

"Are you inside the camera node? Can you turn the cameras they pass off and on?" I asked Jolene.

"Do I look like I just stepped off the assembly line?" she said, sounding huffy. "Of course I'm in. I can hide the cats' incursion. It'll look like the system is experiencing a flicker-glitch."

I wasn't sure *flicker-glitch* was a real term in sophisticated security systems, but I understood it. Jolene's extrapolated floor plan grew in the corner of my face shield just above where it disappeared into my neck gasket.

Spy moved along one hallway. Maul took the other, their cam visuals side by side on my faceplate. When the cats came to doorways or signs, they stopped and sat up, angling their cams so we could see. They found storage for linens, cleaning supplies, a laundry, and a hallway marked as containing pool, lockers, and exercise room.

The cats also found humans.

Even at night, there were a few people moving here and there, wearing casual clothes and boots, clean-looking and smelling, no weapons. Each time the cats sensed a human, they raced into a different hallway or up or down a flight of stairs. Our floor plans were solidifying. And while the cats hadn't been spotted so far, we were pressing our luck.

I heard a sound, not through my comms, and froze. I lowered the volume on my speakers, softened my armor into silent mode, and activated the Chameleon skin enviro invisi-mode, blending me into the landscape. A human form moved through the dark, crunching grass less than twenty meters from me, a flashlight in hand, aimed at the ground and then up into the trees.

"Sentry. Heading my way," I whispered. "Going silent."

Sharp shadows cut through the night, interfering with my lowlight vision. I made out something hanging on a strap. Automatic long rifle. It was the first sign of pickets outside the bunker. She was in cloth clothing—not armor—and she wore an old-fashioned-looking, single-ocular head-set.

I eased behind a trunk and raised my faceplate so the camo would hide my heat signature and blend me into the background. If her ocular was low-light, I was okay. If it had an IR component, I was toast. I glanced at my ATV. It had good enviro camo, which worked well enough in daylight or low-light, but it wasn't top-of-the-line. The heat signature of the small electric engine was still a vibrant red in infrared. If the sentry bumped into it by accident, there would be no hiding it. Also no hiding the tracks it had made getting here; flattened grass would be a dead giveaway. I bent and lifted a stick from the ground. A smaller twig snapped off.

The guard swung the light more slowly. Moved my way.

When the light swung away from me, I threw the stick. It *shushed* through the air. Made a subdued *thump* when it landed in the grass.

The guard turned and followed the sound. Stopped, made a careful detour around nothing that I could see, and then resumed. I figured the detour was to avoid a landmine. The sentry inspected the area where the stick landed. I heard a plastic *click*, and a woman's voice said, "There's nothing out here but dead grass, rat-sign, and rabbit crap, Marvin. And it stinks like dead bodies. Who the hell is burying the failures? They need to dig deeper."

"I'll pass your complaint up the line to the commander," Marvin said wryly.

The female sentry turned away. "You do and I'll be dead, but I'll take you with me first. I'm coming back in. Over."

"Charlie says you can take him with you. You'd go out screaming with pleasure."

She laughed. "Tell him I said to shove it up his butt."

"Check out the burial site before you head back. See if the rats have been digging in it again."

"Fuck that, Marvin. Dead's dead. Let the rats have dinner." She clicked off. Paused. Stopped. Her flash went dark, giving me a clearer view in my own low-light. She studied the area, stepping in place, scanning 360 degrees. And turned toward my ATV.

"What the . . . ?" She inspected the area with the flash. Turned it back off. Walked slowly toward the small armored unit. I tensed. I couldn't let her talk to Marvin again. I couldn't let her go back to the bunker. I activated my left sleeve. I didn't want to kill her.

I didn't.

But I had to.

She clomped toward the ATV. When she reached it, she bent forward. A foot from me. Her hand bumped the vehicle. She jerked back. Fast as a snake, I shot my right hand out and snatched the headset off her, then kicked out, hitting her knee. A series of cracks sounded, and she fell onto me. My left arm went around her throat. Tightened. I pressed the button on my armor to full hardening.

Other than a pained *oooff*, she was silent as my Dragon Scale sleeve cut off her air. Her legs kicked, ramming the ATV. The tree. My armored shins. She was taller than I was, heavier. But the armor made the difference. I crushed the headset and dropped it, grasping my elbow with my free arm to increase the pressure.

She wrenched. Twisted. Threw her weight against me. Her chest heaved as it tried to draw a breath that would never come. Fingers clawed. Scrabbling at my glove.

Tears gathered in my eyes.

Her arms dropped. I didn't let go. A single tear spilled down my cheek.

She stopped fighting.

Something stabbed, sharp, into my groin. Again. Again. Somehow, she had grabbed a knife. Stupid move against armor. She was supposed to give up and die. Should have been dead already. Nanobots keeping her oxygenated?

She kept stabbing. I felt some of the little scales the armor was constructed of slip out of place. Just a fraction. My suit sent me an alert.

"Shining?" Jolene asked, turning up the volume on my speakers. "Sugah? You okay? Your suit cam shows—Cupcake. Shining is not alone. Repeat, she is under attack."

The stabbing continued.

"On the way."

Something at the stabbing site gave. I didn't think it was possible, but the fail-proof armor had a weak spot even when hardened. I breathed out a laugh. It sounded odd. Maybe a little crazy. I pressed my other hand against the side of the guard's head and shoved-twisted.

I heard a dull crack, loud in the silence. I kept twisting. More pop-cracks reverberated into the night. Her head turned all the way around to face me. Dead eyes met mine.

I held her there, staring into lifeless eyes.

Time passed.

"Shining?" Cupcake asked, softly.

I had felt her approaching but I couldn't look away from the eyes of the guard I'd killed. Brown eyes. Dead brown eyes.

"Shhhhiiiining . . ." Cupcake said.

I couldn't think what to do. My brain was still on shocked-numb-kill mode.

Standing in the dry grass of the bunker. Cradling her at my chest.

"You can let go, Shining," Cupcake said, oh so gently. "I got her."

"Okay. I can do that." I released my sleeve, softened my armor. But I didn't let her go. I held her close. Staring into her eyes.

Gently, Cupcake eased her from me. I let her reposition my limbs like a doll on a shelf, arms at my sides. When she fully held the dead sentry, draped over one arm, her suit doing the work, she said, "Jolene. Shining is okay. I'm going to toss the body on a landmine, but we need to get out of here. We've alerted someone. We'll pull back into the brush."

"Copy that," Jolene said.

I bent and picked up the crushed headset. Placed it around the woman's mangled neck.

"I'm tossing the body onto a mine," Cupcake repeated, her blue eyes on mine. "Then we'll retreat."

"Okay." I watched as Cupcake moved through the grasses. Adjusted her armor. Threw the body. And fell face-down as the guard with brown eyes tumbled through the air and dropped. The mine exploded.

An instant later, blood and a small sliver of tissue hit my face shield. I watched as it slid down my face plate. Already cooled in the low-light view.

A hand touched my elbow. Cupcake guided me into the passenger seat of the ATV. Slowly, she backed it along my previous track, behind a boulder big enough to blend with the ATV camo. She turned off the electric engine. I didn't look at her. She didn't look at me.

"It's harder when you're up close like that," she said. "When you can see their eyes."

"Brown eyes. She had brown eyes." I took a breath that hurt to inhale and opened my face shield. The night air was cold on my face. "I could have tied her up and taken her with us. Transitioned her. At least she'd have been alive."

"And they would have looked for her harder, found our tracks, and been able to calculate numbers. They would have been more alert for an attack. Now they have a body and a logical explanation of why she's dead. They won't look for us. You made the right choice."

"Bloody hell." I scratched my fingernails through my hair, which I knew was a stress tell for me. Reaching to my groin, I manually repositioned the mini-scales. They would need some work. The armor hadn't failed, but interestingly for armor that was advertised as having no weak points, also wasn't perfect. "I'll have some bruises. She was strong." My voice sounded odd. Stiff and dead as the brown-eyed woman.

I shoved the image away. Touched my suit into a more comfortable mode. Tried to focus on the pictures and readouts. "I'll think about this—about her—later. Where are we on the Op?"

Mateo said, "We still don't know where Evelyn is."

I steadied my breathing. Without looking at her, I said, "Thank you, Cupcake. You can return to position."

"You're welcome. Anytime."

I felt her moving away. I remembered to breathe. Stared at the screens to figure out what I was seeing. Cats. Right. Cats.

Maul was at a "T" intersection of hallways, a staircase to the right. To the left was a heavy-duty honeycombed hemplaz carbon-fiber composite door—damaged, warped, repaired, but shut. It was marked as Admin Suites. Maul sniffed, and must have smelled something he found upsetting. In the edge of his cam, I saw his hair lift out, standing on end.

As if sending out a call for assistance, he said, *"Orr-rowmerow."*

Spy raced to join him, and standing shoulder to shoulder, they studied what they could see of the hallway and the narrow crack at the base of the door. They sniffed steadily, touching noses often, conferring.

"Admin Suites," I said, sounding almost normal. The cats were on the lowest level. The safest place to be in many ways, protected by the floors above. "Spy, what does it smell like?"

She sent a memory vision to me, one that was upside down, from when she infiltrated the truck filled with Warhammer's people. Spy had been lying across the knees of a man as he scratched her belly. One of the faces was One-Eyed Jack, another Clarisse Warhammer. All the cats had eaten from the bodies of Warhammer's dead thugs, but Spy was the only cat who had been in close proximity to the queen herself. Only Warhammer and her lover Jack had escaped after we fought off their assault.

"Mrow. Siss. Kah," she said again. *Invaders. Dangerous.* And *kah,* the word we had decided upon to mean *enemy queen.* It meant she smelled Warhammer's nanobots. And Warhammer herself.

As if the scents were disgusting, Spy sniffed loud and long, and hacked. It was the same sound as coughing up a hairball. "There are a lot of them in there, aren't there?" I asked her. "In the suites. The queen and her primary mate. And lots of thralls."

"Hhhhah mmm," she said, confirming my guess.

We had gotten lucky. We'd found Warhammer's nest. And we had gotten unlucky. It was in the best-protected site in the bunker, at the bottom level, behind what looked like a modified blast door. There was no way in except with human intervention and, considering the damage to the door, maybe heavy bombardment.

"Spy, can you get an eye down to the crack between

the door and the floor and see anything?" I asked.

A moment later, I got a vision of several pairs of shoes and one pair of dark-skinned human feet, the toenails painted in glittery purple. From down there, I was able to pick up a bit of sound over Spy's mic. "Mateo, can you increase the volume?"

"Affirmative."

The sound went from fuzzy to clear.

"She isn't coming out of it." Warhammer's voice, bored and dismissive. "I won't feed another mindless whiner. End her."

"Can you get us visuals from any cams inside the admin suites?" I asked Jolene.

"They seem to be on a different node," she said. "Working on it."

"No. Please. She'll come around," an unknown voice said from under the door. Male. Bronx accent. "Just let me work with her another week. Please—"

Blood splattered across the floor. Splattered again. And again. Pulsing out in a steady rhythm. The body attached to the purple-painted toenails fell. Bounced. Still spurting blood. Spy caught a view of the face of a Black woman. Her throat had been slit. Blood pulsed out from the carotid. Then it dribbled. And stopped.

In the background I could hear a man sobbing softly. Two pairs of shoes headed toward the door. "When you finish weeping like a child, clean that up and dispose of it outside," Warhammer said. "Jack, bring in the next batch of people to be incorporated. This is taking too long and we're losing too many."

Spy rose off the floor. The two cats separated and darted away, disappearing into the dark.

"That was . . ." Mateo didn't finish his sentence.

"Yeah. It was," I said softly. Warhammer was making thralls fast and not helping them along with med-bay protocols. Some were dying in transition.

On my screen, I followed the progress of the cats as they explored. At one corner, Spy found a stairway going up, marked Level 2 on a bright blue sign. Maul also found a staircase up. Working separately, they found the main command center, marked MCC; storage for armor and munitions; a medical department; and lots of unmarked doors. There were few traces of rats here, but signs of a lot of human activity. The cats dodged people several times, darting into shadows.

After exploring the rest of Level 2, Maul joined Spy on the other side of the compound, and keeping a sharp eye out for more cameras and people, they slinked up the stairs to the upper level, Level 1.

On this side of the compound there was only the faintest old scent of rat. Instead there was the stench of sweat, urine, cooked food, sex, and moldy showers and latrines that hadn't been properly cleaned. Spy disapproved of the complicated tang, and sent me a scent-vision of the different smells of many people, an equal mixture of male and female, healthy and sick. The sick scent was the pong of humans transitioning into thralls.

"Barracks for the hoi polloi," Jolene said, sounding chipper. "If Evelyn is enthralled to Warhammer, this is where she'll be."

Unfortunately, there were a lot of technologically sophisticated cameras, probably multi-spectrum. "Jolene? Cams?"

"On it, Sugah," she said. One of the cameras rotated away from the cats, as if something had caught its attention. The other cam followed. "Looks like we got more than one security hub. This is fun."

And dangerous, I thought. "Spy, you and Maul circle this level fast and head back."

The cats took another turn, peering around. Their tactical-vest cams adjusted to an even dimmer light. They trotted that way and Spy caught the stench of filthy human bodies, the reek of rotting blood, death, and despair. They followed the stink and peeked into a narrow passage. It was murky here, twilight, but the floor was clean. No rat droppings. There were doors along the corridor, three to each side. A sign Maul caught on his camera read Stockade.

"If Evelyn is not enthralled and is a prisoner," I said, "this is where she'll be. Can you see into the cells?"

The cats touched heads again, communicating.

"In case you're wondering," Jolene said, "I'm thinking they got someone watching the cameras now, and they noticed my lil' tricks. I'm altering the glitches." The security cams rotated, stuttered, and stopped. "Security in the stockade is offline, but Spy, you make it quick."

At the far end of the stockade's narrow passage, two human guards were playing cards, arguing about the rules. Neither was watching the dim corridor. Spy appeared in Maul's camera as she slinked along one prison wall. There were six doors, constructed of heavy-duty clear hempglass, not quite the quality used for war and space, but good enough to hold prisoners. Spy turned her chest cam toward each door as she passed.

In the middle cell on the left was the former second-in-command of the USSS *SunStar*, Captain Evelyn Raymond. "That's her," I said. I wouldn't have recognized her except by her tattered, blood-stained uniform.

Mateo growled, a sound worthy of one of the cats.

Evelyn was vastly different from her military photographs—emaciated, thinning gray hair, her skin a sickly pallor, showing bruises and poorly healed scars. None of that should have happened had she been transitioned. Nanobots would have made her younger and healthy and forced her to be on Warhammer's side, not gaunt and in prison.

I remembered the smell of the severed finger Warhammer had sent to me. It had led me to believe Evelyn had been transitioned into a thrall.

Spy studied Evelyn, and so did I. Her fingers had been broken and not set, allowed to heal out of place—the nine she had left, that is. The stump of the tenth was swollen, freshly healed skin at the amputation site.

If Warhammer *had* transitioned Evelyn, why was the captain in pain? Could nanobots be directed by the queen to harm a thrall?

I remembered Cupcake changing personality because I had needed a secretary, a warrior, and a badass right-hand woman. She had become that within hours. Warhammer needed a hostage.

Thrall or not, Evelyn was a trap.

Well that bloody sucks.

Maul let out a *"Sisssss,"* which meant he was unhappy, and Spy looked around, her cam catching his face. His lips were curled back to flash his canines, meaning he was feeling more than simple annoyance. Spy seemed to gather something from him, and she ran past the arguing guards, who never saw her.

Maul went the other direction. Spy darted into a passage with a door on the end and two others bracketing it. She angled her camera to reveal each door's purpose: Kitchen, Bakery, Prep.

Spy pushed her way inside the bakery; it opened with little more than a touch. Lights started to brighten inside. A dozen rats turned to stare at her. *"Mehshh!"* Heart pounding, she turned tail and shoved back into the hall, speeding into the dark.

Maul came around an intersecting hallway and together they raced along the corridor, looking for more stairs up, looking for high ground the way cats looked for tall trees, a way out. Spy was in hair-raised cat-terror mode. I tried to offer advice, but I couldn't get through the fright in her brain to tell her to go down any stairs she found to get away.

The overlapping panic, mental impressions, and the shaky video footage were making me nauseous and dizzy. Spy's brain was a wash of color, scent, and nightmare-like fear. I pulled back mentally and studied the 3D floor plan coming together on my helmet screen.

Eventually the cats' terror was washed away by exhaustion, and they stopped together, huddled in a dark corner. They had outraced the rats. For now.

Maul pressed a pocket on Spy's tac vest and used his teeth to pull out a container of water. Together they turned it top side up, and Maul pressed the small lever that opened it. They both drank until the liquid was gone.

Through the grasses came a whispering sound. Shushing, like wind across the face of the bunker, except the air was still. Assuming it was someone coming to check on the guard I had killed, I stepped behind the rock and the ATV. To one side I saw grass bending and waving, whispering soft threats, but I could see nothing.

The grasses pressed forward, falling flat, then another wave. A group of six rats, walking abreast, appeared. Behind them six more. And six more. They passed by me as if I wasn't standing there. And disappeared. But I could hear them squealing and grunting only a few meters ahead.

They were eating the brown-eyed guard.

I clenched my jaw and turned my attention to the cats.

Maul pawed the small water container down the hall and watched it bounce. Then he sprayed the wall beside them with his scent. Spy added hers. Maul chuffed-growled out a sound that I was sure meant, *This place is ours.*

Forcing my mind away from the rats, I watched the cats. "You've got this," I murmured to Spy. "Slow down. See what's on this level. And when you find stairs, go down, not up."

Spy ignored me, licked her front paw to show me how calm and collected she was, and sauntered along the hallway. *Crazy cat.*

A few paces down was a blast door, similar in shape to the airlocks on space-worthy vessels. It was marked with the word WIMP / TS Clearance.

WIMP. Weakly Interactive Massive dark energy Particles. *TS.* Top secret?

My insides clenched before I could control the reaction.

Below the label were the words *Tier 5 Security Measures required to enter. Palm print and retina scans are compulsory.*

According to the emerging map, this doorway led into a central three-story space that had no other doors. Someone had been trying to get into the room, demoing the security plate and the wall. The palm-and-retina scanner was in pieces on the floor, with a lot of other debris, including heavy-duty, honeycombed hemplaz carbon-fiber composite sheeting that hadn't been dense enough to withstand what looked like an attack by a small rocket. Exposed behind the damage were walls built from ballistic armor, the kind on starship hulls. The blast door was undamaged.

This was the entrance to their power source. Or, if the rumors were true, a massive weapon. A planet killer.

"Bloody damn," I whispered. "Mateo, you seeing what I'm seeing?"

"Affirmative. If Warhammer figures out how to get inside, she might get her hands on an Earth killer. And the presence of WIMP power means we can't use the Simba's city-killer to take the bunker down. It could detonate."

Which would not only do irreparable harm to the planet, it would also attract the Bugs.

I said to Spy, "We have what we need. Retreat."

"*Hhhhah mmm,*" Spy replied, and the two cats headed back down a set of stairs toward their air shaft, a stealthy trek by a different route across the underground compound. They passed offices, more barracks, and food stores that the rats hadn't found yet.

They passed the bunker's main entrance through a series of blast doors, and a loading bay and garage with dozens of ATV-like mini-tanks, a couple dozen civilian vehicles, and the stench of leaking batteries and diesel fuel.

It was getting close to morning, and the cats had a close call with two humans. They sped up their exfil to the escape air shaft.

Using the ropes, they made their way back up the shaft, pulling the ropes behind them. When they were both back at the surface, they dropped the ropes behind the tree, but left them tied, and followed their own scent trail through the grass. Spy stopped when she smelled the remains of the sentry and caught sight of the rats feasting. She hissed and marked the spot with her scent, claiming it.

I opened a hemplaz bucket of water, and though they gave me fierce stares, both cats jumped in, dunking themselves thoroughly to kill any of Clarisse's nanobots they had picked up. Wet and stinking of cat, they then jumped into the small four-wheeler I was driving, and I could finally relax. To show my appreciation I helped them out of their soaked tac vests and rubbed them down with towels. As I worked I said, "You are amazing cats. The best hunter, fighter, infiltrator cats in the history of all cats."

Spy purred, emitting a sense of satisfaction and pride. Maul lifted a leg to groom his privates, showing his mate that he had even more attributes than just being a successful hunter-fighter cat. Spy seemed overly interested in his display.

"Stop that," I said. "Gross."

Maul hacked with amusement.

I poured fresh water into plastic bowls, and opened two cans of super-expensive salmon. They chowed down, and I resisted petting them. When they wanted my attention, they would tell me. Otherwise, I was asking for claw and fang scars. They were not pets. They were equals. Or maybe they were in charge. Once I realized they were sentient and capable of group mental communication, I had never been completely certain of our hierarchy, and maybe it was best that I not find out. Ever.

The cats stopped eating and pricked their ears, staring out into the night. Moments later, I heard an electric engine in the distance, a soft hum of tires on gravel and grass.

I adjusted my helmet's face shield and saw an ATV with two cats on the dash. Cupcake was driving, she and Amos both wearing Dragon Scale exoskeleton anti-recoil armor like mine, and they were laden with weapons. Cupcake gave me a military-style head jut and a halfhearted salute and turned her vehicle around, a clear indication I was supposed to follow them. In the distance I heard the faint hum of the Simba running on silent mode, which meant Mateo was back in his battle tank.

Cats on the narrow dashes of both vehicles, we made our way down the overgrown road, then to a wider road, where we rendezvoused with Mateo, piloting the Simba. The battle tank moved quickly, silently, and efficiently, and our glorified golf carts couldn't keep up. At the next intersection, Mateo opened the Simba's front hatch, extended his warbot's telescoping legs, and picked up our four-by-four vehicles, placing them side by side on the flat top near one of the Simba's rear hatches.

Far down the road, visible through the dead trees, we saw the flashing lights of the Hand of the Law. Before I could react, Mateo shoved the Simba's discrete legs down and lifted the tank treads off the ground. He turned the battle tank off into the trees and down into a deep gulley where he went silent and still. On the street, the cops' patrol cars roared by—old models, running on diesel, engines loud enough to muffle a marching band. The flashing lights slowed, stopped, and turned around. They traveled up and down the road, back and forth, searchlights sweeping the bare trees.

Jolene said into our comms, "I got into the local law's communication system. They had a notification from the military that something big and unregistered was moving up the road. Y'all sit tight. As per CO Mateo's previous order. I got to get into the corporate sat systems and make you look like a glitch, so the military will call them off."

Bloody hell. The military, the Gov., and corporate military complexes had been in each other's pockets since before the war, and with no oversight it had only gotten worse since the war ended.

My heart was racing, and I felt a little nauseous. If the military caught us with the Simba, we'd end up in an underground jail and never see the light of day again. If we lived through the confrontation. Which wasn't likely.

Minutes passed.

Jolene said, "They sent up some aerials with cameras. Keep it dark."

"Roger that," Mateo said.

I tapped a private channel to Mateo. "Why here? Why now?"

"We must have triggered a sensor before we turned off the highway and took this tertiary road. Which we did to bypass the border checkpoints."

Half an hour later, the cops pulled off and turned down the side road, spotlights shining into the trees as the rising sun made the shadows long and blacker than the night had been. Then they pulled away, emergency lights going dark.

"Okay, CO Sugah. The military's sensors are now showing a glitch, but y'all can't stay on the roads. You're gonna have to travel overland some. I've got topo maps, and I can keep you from falling off a cliff, but it ain't gonna be a fun trip home."

I punched the button to remove my armor, stored it in the ATV, and dressed in black layers from the stuff Cupcake had packed into my gear bag. Prewar, the trip would have taken maybe two hours. Three with traffic. *This is gonna suck,* I thought.

I was right.

Thanks to the change in route, the piss-poor back roads, and having to ford mucky river beds whose bridges had been washed away in floods over the years, it took us two-and-a-half nights to get back to the junkyard. For the most part, we had to hunker down and hide in the ATVs by day, trying to sleep. We were sunburned, dehydrated, and miserable when we pulled in, arriving after midnight, having been gone for five nights and four days. We were tired, sleepless, gripey, and stank to high heaven.

In the office, I tossed my armor into the donning station where the receptacles for body fluids would be sanitized and the entire suit treated to a decontam for my own nanobots. Exhausted, I wanded myself halfway clean, gave all the cats kibble and water, and fell into bed. Maul curled against my spine and Spy draped around my head like a crown. I had a feeling that was less happenstance and more symbolic, but I was too tired to care.

*
*

At four a.m., a rooster crowed and woke me. It wasn't the first time. The rooster had gotten out of the henhouse and taken off into the junkyard where, I assume, he ate toxic bugs and chased the hens when they got out. And he crowed. I said, "Gomez, mute all outside noise."

"Muted," the AI said in his calm voice. I shoved Spy off my pillow, rolled over, and went back to sleep.

At ten a.m., I woke to comfortable temps, the AC not yet running in the background. I completed my ritual mourning for Harlan and remembered, one by one, all the people I had killed, ending with the brown-eyed sentry. She hadn't deserved to die. Several hadn't deserved to die. But they were gone, nonetheless.

I rolled out of bed, let out the cats, hit *start* on the coffeemaker, and spent enough time in the personal toilette compartment to actually feel cleanish without the use of water. A full body wanding took time, and when I was done, I still had to vacuum up the dead skin cells and hair. Hygiene in the barren stone desert of West Virginia was difficult and time consuming.

I sniffed the clothes I had left hanging over the stall door days ago, decided they didn't stink too bad, and dressed, then finger-combed hair goop through my short, sun-bronzed hair, slathered sunscreen over my brown skin, and opened the door to the office. The smell of coffee, faux bacon, and eggy goo with peppers and garlic was a sour spicy scent that wasn't entirely pleasant. And there were people. Even after all these weeks, it was still a shock to my system to see humans in my office-home. Thralls had no sense of personal space, so they seldom knocked, had figured out how to get inside no matter how well I secured the doors, and were here every single morning with my breakfast and their itinerary.

Every. Single. *Bloody*. Day.

Cupcake dished up our plates; Amos poured our coffee. Tuffs, the pride's Guardian Cat queen, was sitting on the back of the Comms chair, and her mate, Notch, sat on the foot of the bed, watching. The tip of Tuffs's tail was twitching, a sign that she was less calm than she appeared. Taking my place at the dinette I had repurposed out of a high-end RV meant turning my back to the cats, which was still difficult to do and required more trust than I normally possessed.

Tuffs had a tortoiseshell coat, eyes the color of spring leaves and forest moss—green things I remembered from before the war. She had strange, bobcat-like tufts on her ears and one gimpy paw that been partially amputated in a junkyard accident. I called her Tuffs because of the ear feathers and because she was so tough. Notch was a solid steel gray with a notched ear from a fight long ago, and was one of the few intact fighter cats who Tuffs allowed to breed.

"Good morning, Sunshine," Cupcake sang as she slid my plate in front of me.

I grunted. Amos grunted too and handed me a cup of hot, strong black coffee. The real thing. Having all this new money meant no more drinking fake coffee, no old stale coffee, no weak coffee that was more water than caffeine, and no fear of running out of coffee, kibble, or water. And that ability to buy stuff was a direct result of Cupcake being in my life. If only she didn't talk so much.

All. The. Time.

Cupcake chattered brightly through the meal and continued the prattle afterward, as she cleaned the office. I started on one set of the quarterly books—for the taxes and the official merch—and Amos restocked the medical supplies in the med-bay. Cleaning included giving the Bug

alien command chair a thorough vacuuming and damp wip-
ing to remove accumulated cat hair. Lately, the cats—who
were led inside in small groups by Tuffs, for reasons I still
didn't understand—had often abandoned my bed in favor
of the Bug ship's extra-large Comm chair, which suited me
just fine, though it was possible their lounging location meant
they were assuming command. With cats, who knew?

"Did you hear a single word I said?" Cupcake demanded.

I looked up from the books, dredging through my un-
conscious memory for her last words. "Veggies in the
greenhouse, some fruit, lots of greens. The old rainwater
storage container on the roof has been patched. The new
water-collection system is ready for cooler, damper weather. And you have a new toy for me." Thirty minutes of
babble condensed into four lines.

"And the part about Mateo?"

"His business," I said, my tone going steely.

"Not so. He's got the hots for Evelyn, and we all know
it. That's why we're going after her. He was in love with her
onboard, during the war. You *know* it," she said, her tone
as unyielding as my own.

I had always wanted Cupcake to stand up to me, to be
her own woman. That desire was coming back to haunt me.

"I'm outta here," Amos said. "It's gonna get all girly."
He levered his big body toward the airlock. "But if you decide to go all girl-on-girl wrestling, call me back in."

"Perve," Cupcake said, but her word sounded all lovey
-dovey.

"Ever' chance I get." He kissed her on the forehead
and lumbered through the airlock, letting out one batch of
cats and letting in another, who instantly started roaming
and familiarizing themselves with the space.

The cats were all juvenile males this time, and Tuffs
gave me a demanding look that cemented my idea about
the cats thinking they were in charge. But she had a point.
My job today would be to stick all eight of the unneutered
juvenile males in the med-bay for a snip-and-tuck. The
males had no idea what was about to happen, and to make
it easier on myself, I reconstituted some goat milk and added a hundredth of a milliliter of illegal Devil Milk.

While I worked I replied to Cupcake, "We have to stop

Clarisse. We have an ethical obligation to rescue Evelyn."

I set the bowl on the floor, and the males came running. Tuffs stretched yoga moves on top of the commander's Bug chair and watched in satisfaction.

I tucked in my earbud and tapped it. "Mateo. Talk to me."

"After going over all the cat-cam footage again, the recce shows we have to go with Plan D," his grating voice said in my ear. "Evelyn is not a thrall. No thrall would be in such bad shape. I'm getting her out. I owe her."

"Or she is a thrall, and Clarisse is torturing her with her nanobots. And before you ask, yes, I think it's possible, and no I will not test my theory on any of you."

Mateo cursed.

For him, Plan A had always been to sneak in and rescue his second-in-command and deploy the Simba's city-killer bomb. It assumed that there weren't many enemy thralls to fight and that Evelyn could be knocked on the head and carted out. Plan B, had Evelyn not been in the bunker at all, had been to just drop in the city-killer to destroy Clarisse and her thralls. Plan C had been a weird combo of an all-out assault and heavy bombardment, based on the probability that Evelyn was a thrall, then using the city-killer threat to negotiate for her release. And then double-crossing Warhammer and deploying the city-killer after we had Evelyn. Now we had a new plan on the table—Plan D, which was like Plan C but without negotiating and without the use of the city-killer. Just infiltrate, get Evelyn, kill Warhammer, and take down everything with different weapons—ones that would not detonate or damage anything WIMP-powered. D ended with me transitioning Evelyn, to heal her with my nanobots.

Plan and A, C, and D required more warriors than we currently had—which is why we needed to recruit the bikers we would be meeting.

I couldn't stop seeing Evelyn's tortured body. Or the blood spurting on the floor of Warhammer's nest. The Black woman's face as seen through Spy's eye beneath the door. Or the brown-eyed guard I had killed. The mutated mega-rats walking in lockstep. Instinct said we had to save Evelyn and kill everything else in that place.

But I also remembered the size of the bunker. And the three-story WIMP room.

As if reading my thoughts, Mateo said, "If there's a WIMP bomb or power source in that bunker, the Simba's city-killer will likely detonate it."

He'd said this before, and I knew it was true. "Options?"

"We can employ other explosive devices to bring down the bunker once we have Evelyn and after we are safely away," Mateo said. There was something in his voice that said he wasn't telling me everything that was going on in the back of his Berger-chipped brain, but I wasn't going to exploit my control over him to demand he tell me. That would be an abuse of power.

I sighed softly. *Explosives. Right.* There weren't enough explosives in our entire arsenal to get through that shielding, and Jolene hadn't been able hack her way through the WIMP door electronically. The Simba—the Suit Initiated Main Battle Tank—and especially its city killer was supposed to be our ace in the hole. People had died for us to get it. And now it was useless.

"Mateo," I said. "Outline Plan D. A version that lets us get away alive."

He chuckled, that grating noise that sounded like rusted pipes being rubbed together. "The Simba has weapons that can take out precision targets at five kilometers using aerial targeting systems. It's equipped with jamming devices to bring down remote aircraft and is mounted with a rail gun and rapidly repositioning blasters that can take down a platoon of warbot-suited warriors. It has precision lasers that can cut through some heavy steel plate like butter. But since we can't use the city-killer because of the WIMP presence . . ." He paused. "We'll have to use bunker busters."

My head came up at that. "You have bunker buster missiles?" I had no clue the Simba had weapons big enough to bust through earth and fortified installations.

"Jolene zaps the security system, we precision infil small teams. Close-quarter combat. Take Evelyn. Kill Warhammer before she knows we've gotten in. Let the bikers remove what they want provided everything is washed down to kill nanobots. Then we take down the bunker safely with the busters. Fire them on a low trajectory, so they don't display on standard sensors or sats and alert the military. And bug the hell out before they find us."

"Okay." I said, hands on my head, hiding my eyes as if not seeing could keep us away from all the pathways to danger and destruction. "You're right. If—and that's a big if—we can get the bikers to help, we'll go with Plan D." Plan D was slightly less suicidal than the others. And . . . *missiles. Bloody damn.*

Mateo blew out a breath. It shrilled like an old-fashioned whistle. "Roger that."

"Somebody talk about the pink elephant in the room. All *this?* Attacking a military bunker? Fighting another queen and her entire nest? Risking our lives? For *love?*" Cupcake said, her tone full of frustration, as if love was the biggest problem we faced. "But fine. As long as you understand that you're taking me and Amos to the negotiations. We already decided."

I shook my head in resignation, picked up the eight sleeping juvie cats, placed them in the med-bay, and punched in the sequence to de-ball them.

Then I set the rest of the office to decontam, killing off any additional nanobots I had left behind in the last few days. I decontaminated every day now.

I had been reinfected with PRC nanobots when we rescued the Simba. The infection had been brutal, as my own bots attacked and destroyed the invaders, and though mine had won, the attack had changed the composition of my nanobots. The cats hadn't shown signs of sickness, but Amos, Cupcake, and Mateo had all been forced back through transition again, simply because they had been close to me. Since then, my people had gotten more ornery, which had given me hope that the humans I had previously enthralled were also less mentally enslaved.

A girl could dream.

Sometimes dreams had consequences.

I stepped into the cool of the morning.

*

*

Autumn in the stone desert of West Virginia was unpredictable, the thermometer shooting up into the thirties Centigrade by day and plunging below zero at night. We all sweated with summer stink when the sun's heat was blaring off the broken stone and the junkyard's metal scrap, and slept under blankets at night, when the temps dropped and froze the water in the cats' bowls. But this abnormally hot day had me itchy, jittery, as if expecting . . . something. Nothing major was supposed to happen today. I had arrangements and timelines for everything, and today was for final discussion, decisions, and packing the flatbed. Yet, my itchy skin and nerves had me expecting trouble.

Somehow *not* having trouble, having to hold it all in, made me more jittery. So I worked, sorting trade goods, sweating the worry off me, keeping occupied until whatever was about to happen, happened. Or didn't.

I scratched at the sweat sliding down my chest as I shoved a case of military handheld blasters into the flatbed. These blasters were third or fourth generation. Kill speed was one-and-a-half seconds at a distance of six meters. At three meters, the kill speed dropped to half. At point blank, it was faster than an eye blink. The blasters' only drawback was that the casing got hot against human skin. These were devised to be held in a fist gloved with battle armor. As trade items went, warriors would salivate over them.

I forced my attention back to paperwork, and considered the new mattress inventory Cupcake had entered onto my old handheld system. "Mattress inventory" referred to the off-the-official-books inventory kept by illegal traders, once upon a time, under their bedroom mattresses. I kept my off-book inventory on the handheld because no sat-links could access it, it was easy to hide, and I could burn the data on it to ashes with the thumbprint biomarker on the side.

As far as the Hand of the Law and the Gov.'s tax assessors were concerned, Smith's Junk and Scrap specialized in the basics: pre-war metal and post-war surplus items like hemplaz, stripped-down military vehicles, and recyclable garbage. In reality—off-book—Smith's was hiding a lot of illegal contraband, stuff the Gov. or the military would confiscate if they found out about it. Then they'd lock me in a

Class Five Containment Center, a prison so far below ground I'd never see daylight again.

Some of this mattress inventory stuff could be used to entice the necessary people to the negotiation table, or so Cupcake had promised. We had a lot of military gear, silver, gold jewelry, real cotton sheets, canned meat, dried beans —stuff people hoarded and hid after the war and was scarce because the military and the Gov. had confiscated so much to use on the front lines, in space-going vehicles, and in low-orbit war planes. And because the cotton market had dried up when the atmosphere changed. Cotton wouldn't grow where it used to. Neither would tobacco, marijuana, hops, grapes, or large-scale crops.

An unnamed female cat walked toward me, her direction unerring, looking to the side as if not seeing me. I didn't look at her either, watching her from my peripheral vision. She walked straight up to me, circled once, and sat on my booted foot. She yawned and stretched her neck. Bored. Her body language said, *I don't see the junkyard queen. And if I did, I'm mean enough to take her.*

Nope.

I shifted my foot slightly. Softly, I said, "If you get up and saunter away now, all the cats watching while you act stupid will think you're fearless. You don't leave, you'll never make it back off the bottom ranks of the pride."

The young cat stood, stretched, showed me her butt as if about to spray to mark territory.

Fast as a snake—or a junkyard queen—I swiped down and picked her up by the scruff of the neck like a kitten, and held her in front of my face. We met eyes, hers vibrant yellow and wide with shock. My voice barely more than a whisper, I said, "Don't play games you can't win, Little Kitten. I'm bigger. I have weapons that outweigh your claws and fangs. And I'm meaner than any junkyard cat you ever met."

Her claws came out and she tried to scratch my arm, but I'd watched Tuffs deal with younglings before. She missed by half a meter. She dangled from my hand, slightly above my head.

"Keep it up and I'll embarrass you in front of your rebel teenaged clowder. Stop now and your life will be easier."

She hissed at me, and I lifted my brows. "You're going to be trouble, Little Kitten," I said. "If Tuffs brings you to me for neutering, I'll oblige, and you will never be a *queen of cats*."

She blinked, thinking, and slowly retracted her claws. She looked down in fake submission and went limp. "Uh-huh. Let's see how you act, going forward. Threat stands."

I wasn't fooled, but I set her on the ground and she shook herself before reacquiring her saunter, as if taking me at the literal meaning of "going forward." She walked away, tail high, an insult in cat body language.

"Not exactly smart," I said, "but not ultra-dumb either. *Maybe* you'll survive to adulthood, but I somehow doubt it."

Little Kitten turned and hissed at me again before slinking around a pile of late-twentieth-century auto bodies. *Stupid cat.* She'd get herself and her pals killed if she went up against Tuffs. Even three-pawed, Tuffs could take the young cat.

A loud *whomp* shook the air, and my nerves had me flinching. I followed the sound-vibration around to Aisle Tango Three to see Mateo. He was pulling more military weapons from a buried shipping container and tossing them up to the desert stone.

When we got back from acquiring the Simba, we had also brought home some full-sized shipping containers that held military and medical hardware. There were weapons. So many weapons: top-of-the-line armor, next-generation blasters, lasers, weapons charging stations, multi-ammo-convertible automatic weapons, Tesla Lockmart IGPs (AKA Antigravity Probe-Lifter-Compactors, AKA AG Grabbers). And there was a container full of Medical Battlefield Bays, or MBBs—specialized triage med-bays—and battlefield-quality medical supplies.

It was stuff the people I would be negotiating with would kill me to obtain. I knew that for a fact because I'd murdered the man I'd taken them from. Marty Morrison had needed killing, but that was beside the point. I'd stared into his eyes while I boiled his innards with my old but functional blaster.

One of the containers I had taken from him held a

thousand blasters, all with serial numbers that would prove they had been stolen. If they went out en masse, they would eventually lead the military to me and my junkyard. Despite the danger, Mateo had removed more cases of the blasters and placed them into the pile for barter. There were nineteen cases, each containing two blasters, each case also holding one multi-method charging station. Counting the case I had tossed on the truck, that made twenty cases, forty blasters.

Also lying in the dust were much bigger cases, each containing an armor suit with all the bells and whistles, and one very large box containing an armor-donning station. It was all the very latest in military equipment. Stolen military equipment. *Traceable* stolen military equipment.

In a separate pile were new high-quality plaz-steel military knives, and excellent quality boots which were hard to come by now that boot-making leather was so scarce due to the near extinction of cattle. There were also heat-retention blankets, ghillie suits, and vast amounts of sunscreen, which was nearly as valuable as water. No one went outside without protection from the sun. The increased radiation from the depleted atmosphere and damaged magnetosphere were directly responsible for the extinction of most animals, and the high rate of cancers. This pile was all mass-produced, desperately needed, and had no traceable serial numbers or built-in trackers that might endanger us.

It should have been heartwarming to see that Mateo had dug out and removed a great quantity of things that would not get me arrested and only a few things that would get me permanently caged. But somehow, I wasn't feeling all warm and cozy. I'd wanted Mateo to be independent, but a Mateo who had grown obsessive over someone not in my nest was disturbing. And the fact that I was disturbed was disturbing too.

"I updated your inventory for the things I've pulled out," Mateo said, his voice grating, as if responding to my unvoiced concerns by ignoring them and yet sounding belligerent at the same time. "Anything else you think we should take for trade?"

I wasn't used to taking other people's thoughts and

feelings into consideration, but it occurred to me that because Mateo was the commanding officer of a starship—even if it was crashed in a junkyard—he had no idea what people who lived in the underbelly of normal society would really want. And we would be dealing with the underbelly of the snake.

I didn't indicate the direction of my thoughts. Instead I said, "How many of the portable triage MBBs do we have?"

"Twelve. You want to give them *med-bays*? Why?"

I'd never understand Mateo's thought processes and military training. He would give current enemies only basic medical supplies to save themselves, yet that same thinking had always been okay with giving potential *future* enemies weapons and ammo which could later be used against us or our allies.

I ran my fingernails against my scalp in frustration. I'd dropped my hat somewhere. My scalp was sweaty. "You want to save Evelyn or you want to bitch about my *bloody damn* methods?" I growled.

"Save Evelyn."

"So shut up, CO Sugah," Jolene said into our comms system. "Evelyn comes first. You said it. So stop bein' a pussy about regs and get with Shining's program."

"Pus—" Mateo went silent.

To forestall what could be the first raging argument in history between a commanding officer of a starship and his sentient AI, I said, "Pack up six triage med-bays and put them on the truck. Make sure at least one is programmed for, and has supplies for, helping people through the transition, and one is a vet-bay. Add in some good Berger chips. They make nice bargaining items, and they don't kill. Keep out ten armor units and the multi-donning station. They'll just fight over them unless we have enough for each club to get at least two suits of armor. We'll take twelve blasters, max. That's not enough for them to kill each other and me over, but enough to convince them I might have value other than raping and the sex trade."

"I thought these were the good guys," Mateo said.

"There are no good guys." I stopped. I wasn't sure if I believed that, but it was enough to shut Mateo up.

"Yup. I agree with Shining, CO Sugah. According to human history there ain't many truly good guys, but the few there were made a big difference," Jolene said. "Like Jesus and Buddah and Gandhi and such."

"Yeah. Well," I said. "We're not dealing with holy men. We'll be dealing with biker clubs. And the meeting is at one p.m. tomorrow, so let's not screw this up by arguing or taking trade items that will bring them to our doorstep."

"Roger that," Mateo said.

"Fine by me, Sugah."

"Good by me," Cupcake said.

"Not that you asked me," Amos added, his tone laconic, "but I want me one o' them blasters to go with my armor. Imma look so cool Cupcake will drool all over me trying to get me out of it."

"I can get you out of your armor in a snap, you doofus, but . . . I only need one part of you free to make me happy. You know. *Happy?*"

"Stop!" I shouted into my mic. "Not another word."

Cupcake tittered. Amos chuckled, sounding lascivious. Mateo said nothing.

"Okay," I said, changing the subject. "Cupcake, what about this new toy you mentioned at breakfast?"

"It's a beauty," she said. "It's a nano detector. Jolene made it in her lab."

"We have activity at the outer perimeter," Mateo interrupted. "ARVACs are airborne."

"Jagger?" Cupcake asked. "You know he's gonna come around sometime."

"Negative," Mateo said, a moment later. "ARVACs indicate an old electric truck. Long bed. Traveling at a manageable thirty-two kilos an hour."

"I got it, Mateo. You take care of that," I ordered, my hand making a circular motion encompassing the trading stuff on the ground. At a dead run I headed back to the office.

Inside, I pressed the small button that allowed me to see the security screens and spotted the old truck as viewed from an ARVAC cam. It was loaded down with big bags and plastic bins and household stuff—a mattress, a recliner, pillows—all strapped down with old flex. It was also towing a fourteen-foot trailer. A shotgun barrel extended out on the driver's side, meaning the driver was riding their own shotgun. There was too much glare to see faces, but I knew who this was and what had happened. As Wanda neared, I felt her desperation and her panic. I felt her awareness of another person in the vehicle. Was she under duress?

"Bloody damn," I whispered. Keeping an eye on the screen, I wanded the sweat off me and dressed in cleaner clothes. Checked on the cats in the med-bay. Four were done. The rest were still being neutered.

Knowing this was going to suck no matter how it went down, I turned off some of the perimeter security measures along the drive so no one got killed by accident and grabbed my comms and my second-gen sunglasses just in case there were enemies along for the ride. I debated carrying weapons, but I knew that there was an appearance of strength to not carrying them, and also that I would be well protected by Mateo, who I could feel moving toward the drive. Weaponless, I walked out of the airlocks and into the hot sun. In the middle of the dirt drive, about twenty meters off the old rutted, pitted road, I stopped.

Cats gathered around my feet, and without looking I knew it was the clowder that had gone with Cupcake and me to Charleston.

The rest of my nest was all around me: Mateo at the juncture of Aisle Tango Three and Aisle Alpha Three now, watching on his suit screens; cats mostly in clowders with a few outliers all heading this way; Cupcake walking toward my flank; Amos taking up a firing position behind the AG grabber.

The old truck turned in, its electric engine silent. Wanda braked about six meters away and turned off the engine. She got out of the vehicle, leaving the door open as she approached. She was wearing a sweat-stained dress and old sneakers without laces. She hadn't had a bath or a personal wanding in a long while. The stink of her body reached me before she did. Her skin was cracked and her hair dry as straw, signs of dehydration.

Behind her, in the windshield, a face pressed close to the old plaz-glass.

Bloody damn.

Wanda had her kid with her. Worse, I could feel the pull, the attraction, the knowledge that the kid was mine too, part of my nest.

What in all the flames of all the hells was I going to do with a kid? And how did this happen? Instantly, a possible explanation presented itself. When she got home from Morrison's Foundry, Metals, and Scrap, Wanda had hugged her kid. Some of my nanobots had transferred during that hug. I should have made sure Wanda showered more thoroughly, washed her hair, changed clothes, changed shoes, before she left Morrison's. I hadn't pushed her to be scrupulously clean. I hadn't done enough to protect her child.

My fault. *I hadn't thought*.

Wanda stopped in front of me, her hands hidden in the folds of her full skirt. "I tried to stay away. But I lost my house when the new mayor decided to put up a housing unit." Her hands bunched into the lank cloth and released it. Bunched and released. "I had no place to stay." Tears gathered in her eyes, but they dried instantly. "I'm falling apart staying away from you. My kid and I were living on the street. So I tracked down Jagger, and he told me how to get here."

I wasn't a kind person by nature, but I knew responsibility. I knew honor, the kind I had learned at Pop's knee and in WWIII fighting with the OMW. And I knew that when I made a mistake—like leaving Wanda alone in Charleston—I had to make it right.

Before I could speak she added, "Jagger said I should bring the most recent intel I uncovered. That it might make you willing to take me in. Take *us* in. I can work. I'm good at secretarial things. Good with accounting of all kinds. I can clean and—"

I raised a hand to stop her. "You're welcome here, Wanda. You and the kid."

Wanda's shoulders started shaking, and I realized she was crying arid, tearless sobs. She was broken inside. She was a thrall, and her queen had left her behind. I was coming to understand that, even with my own newly mutated nanobots, my thralls still wanted to be with me, and some of them would find it impossible to resist the need for a queen.

Bloody sodding damn.

"Pull your vehicle up to the office. Cupcake will find you a place to stay and some supplies."

Wanda gagged and dropped to her knees as if my words had slammed her down. Or were lifesaving. Maybe both.

I'd been mostly a kid when I made my slow, dangerous way across the country to Smith's Junkyard and Scrap. Along the way I had been close to dead more than once. Getting here, to safety, had been a huge relief. "Wanda, it's okay," I said gently. "I'm sorry I left you there so long."

"Sugah," Jolene said into my earbud, "Wanda gave us good intel while she was in Charleston. We got stuff on Marconi and all his young'uns. And she was searching for who's on the take in the local law, which is prolly what she's brought with her."

"Wanda, you were . . . serving me in Charleston. In a big way," I said, guided by Jolene's words. I walked close and touched her shoulder with one fingertip. "All that information you sent was invaluable. And even if it had been crap, I'd still have welcomed you here."

Wanda leaned into me and hugged my thighs, weeping.

Yet. What if . . . ? I was paranoid. Which might keep us alive.

I tried to figure out where to put my hands on Wanda and finally patted her head. She hugged my legs tighter.

At the truck, two little feet landed on the dirt, visible beneath the open door. Sneakers in a faded blue. Bare legs. A towheaded kid peeked around the door and met my eyes. Bright blue eyes in a very dirty face.

I sighed and held out my hand. The kid raced to me but threw himself—herself?—against their mother's back. They—the kid—were wearing filthy clothes that might once have been shorts and a T-shirt. Gently he-she-they reached out a small grubby hand and held it two centimeters away from my leg. Sighing, I took the hand. The kid and Wanda both sighed with me, then slumped against my thighs.

I might be paranoid, but I checked for foreign nanobots, just in case Warhammer had found her, enthralled her again, and sent her. But the nanos on and in Wanda and the kid were all my old ones, the ones from before my recent PRC nanobot infection. I had hoped that my new transition had been enough to end my thralls' dependence on me. I had been wrong. And now, my touching would infect them with my new improved nanos. *Bloody damn*.

"I gotcha, Wanda," Cupcake said, sliding a hand under her elbow. "We've been saying how much we need another secretary to handle the front desk and the calls."

"If we'd a known you were in trouble, Honey Cake," Jolene said, her voice coming from the speaker system near the driveway, "we'd a sent for you ages ago. You done good, gal. Real good."

That should have been my line and I knew it. "Make sure they have everything they need," I said. "Supper tonight in the office, Cupcake. Something special?"

Cupcake pulled the two to their feet and away from me, leading them down the dusty drive into the junkyard. Amos drove their truck into an open place near the guest quarters and began unloading it.

Pulling my mic around, I spoke softly into the comms system, so Wanda couldn't hear me. "Cupcake. We need cams on them." She didn't reply, but I knew she had heard.

The housing was something new to the junkyard—three cargo containers on Aisle Alpha Two. There was a fancy one for Amos and Cupcake, and two had more minimal supplies: water, ready-to-eat meals, basic furniture, and a personal toilette compartment. One had hidden cameras inside to watch the guests. It was a guesthouse or prison, whichever we needed, with just a turn of the locking mechanism.

"Jolene," I said, "look at the intel Wanda says she brought. Add it to ours. When Cupcake is free, get her to look for long-term housing for Wanda in Naoma. The kid will need to go to school, and they don't have to live on-site twenty-four seven."

"Gotcha, Shining Sugah."

Cats around my feet, I decided to go over the inventory in the smallest, dirtiest storage shed in the junkyard, which looked as if it would fall in with a gentle wind. But the ramshackle appearance was false; it was built like a vault. And like a vault, it was packed full of gold and gems in the form of jewelry. My Pops had left me a fortune, and I had never known about it until Cupcake arrived. If she had been paid a salary, I'd owe her a raise.

Spy, watching me from the shade of an overhang, sent me an image of a slab of salmon, presented to Cupcake.

I breathed out a laugh. If Cupcake wanted money, she knew where the stuff was located better than I did. But . . . maybe I owed money and approval and awards or something. The Outlaws gave patches and women and status to made-men. And status and money to female made-men. The military gave money and rank and pretty little medals. I'd have to think about that.

In my earbud, I heard Cupcake chatter as she led Wanda and the kid away. "Amos will bring in your stuff. Hydrate, sleep, clean up, eat, whatever. Supper is at six thirty."

I hadn't felt Warhammer's nanobots on Wanda or her kid. So far as I could tell, neither had been transitioned away from me. The presence of the kid suggested Wanda wasn't here to infiltrate and observe. But her timing *was* unsettling.

When Cupcake left Wanda and the kid, I tapped my mic and said, "So I wasn't being paranoid at the timing of Wanda's appearance, Cupcake?"

"You weren't alone, Shining," she replied into the comms system. "It's fishy as week-old cod. Jolene, security system on?"

"Video and audio on, Cupcake, darlin'. The kid's name is Alex. I'm searching through archives to see if I can find a birth record."

Mateo said into the comms, "Shining is popular this week. Outlying systems indicate we have another visitor. Male. Riding a motorcycle. Good thing you left the outer perimeter weapons system offline." If his vocal cords could sound sly, they would have.

Jagger? *That* could make me feel weird.

Mateo said, "We have ARVAC readouts and vid."

"I'm listening."

"Sensors suggest he's on his OMW bike, the one equipped with a miniaturized MPP. Muters on the engine." Muters changed the sound of a Harley, creating an infiltrator mode, a soft snore rather than the full-throated war-bike roar. "Enviro visual shielding is functional but not active. Our sensors are better. He is alone as far out as the sensors can detect.

"The One Rider bike is mounted with the same weapons as his first visit: one 9-millimeter Heckler & Koch MP8 Universal Machine Pistol, two 9-millimeter Heckler & Koch MP8 machine pistols. As per visuals, he is not armored but wearing kutte. Jeans. Two additional semiautomatic weapons on his person, make unknown. Knife in a hip sheath."

"I'm unarmed," I replied. "Are you in position to take him down should he instigate hostile actions or prove to be an unfriendly?"

"Affirmative and with pleasure."

"Yeah, well, don't shoot him just for fun."

Mateo made that grinding snorting sound of laughter. If the warbot warrior decided to shoot Jagger, there was nothing I could do to stop him.

*

*

The bike turned in and puttered up the drive to me. It was Jagger, on his official Harley—the one he rode as enforcer to McQuestion, the war chief and vice president of the Outlaw Militia Warriors—and his bike and clothing told me that this was an official visit. A black leather jacket was strapped on the bike, probably from when he started out on a cold ride at dawn. He was wearing his kutte with all its patches over a sweat-soaked T-shirt, sweat-stained jeans, and riding boots. He wore fingerless riding gloves, a helmet, and a neckerchief against the sun. He was sporting a week-old beard I could see beneath the telescoping modified faceplate, the hemplaz shield splattered with the guts of the desert's toxic mutated bugs who were still looking for a place to overwinter. He also carried all the weapons Mateo had described.

And he was everything I remembered. Big. Lean. Shoulders like a slab of concrete. Dark haired. Bloody gorgeous.

The bike came to a stop. His feet dropped to the dirt. The bike went silent.

Through the faceplate his eyes met mine. My insides clenched as if we were in bed together and I was ready. So ready. But I relaxed my posture as if I had no cares in the world and said nothing. Jagger was here without an invitation, without an order from me, without notifying me first. It was the surprise assault of an unexpected business meeting, OMW style, and with the negotiations coming up, that might mean anything.

"Asshole," I greeted him calmly.

Still straddling the bike, he pushed up the gut-smeared faceplate and grinned through his beard. "McQuestion sends his regards to Little Girl, Shining Smith, made-man, daughter of the war chief and then the international president, Bill Smith."

So. McQuestion knew my name and lineage. It was going to happen eventually, and wasn't surprising, but it was still sucky.

"Greetin's and felicitations," a Southern voice said over the speaker system. Jolene was sticking her nose in.

At my feet, Spy let out a loud *"Siss Mrower! Orrrow-merow,"* telling me that though she knew this man and had fought mutual enemies with him, right now he was an invader and bad news all around. To Spy, something was off about him—anger in his body language, tension in his face, probably something she could detect in his scent.

Yeah. Not my Jagger. *McQuestion's* Jagger.

From my other side came Tuffs's decidedly lower-pitched *"Baaaahr."* *This place is ours.* Cats were all around me now, weaving or staring or hiding in ambush, eyes on Jagger.

Into my ear, Mateo said, "Passive systems just pinged. He's wired. He may be under suspicion by his boss."

That was even more bad and meant I needed to step carefully. I let a tiny smile move my lips. "Asshole. Logan Jagger, national enforcer to McQuestion. Little Girl attends you. But if you move wrong, you will be struck down and killed and your innards given to the cats. We clear?"

"Crystal."

Tuffs said, *"Kkkkk."* *Dead humans. Good protein.* The rest of the cats echoed her, *"Kkkkk"* coming from all around me and resounding into the junkyard.

Mateo said into my comms, "One tiny cam on his bike, facing you. Someone's getting a real good look at you, Shining."

"Why did you identify yourself as Heather on my last

visit?" Jagger growled. "And where is this boss you claim to have?"

As lies went, that was a good one, questions that might keep him alive if the cam and the mic meant he was under threat. I pursed my lips, thinking. Popped a hand on a hip and said, "Intel said MSA was moving in. I'm outta the loop on OMW operational protocols and the current organizational situation. I had no idea if you were compromised. Still don't. So I lied. It's not a killing offense." I grinned briefly. "Not most of the time."

The tension in Jagger's face eased. My words told him that I had caught on and he could relax some. He said, "Red's Old Lady has been contacting leaders of the biker clubs and companies all over the eastern half of the US for a parley."

"Eastern" meant east of the Mississippi. Most of the land to the west was barren desert, ruins, and PRC bots, with a few outposts of civilization and the military still fighting the good fight against decreased rainfall, floods, and autobots that built more bots out of the remains of cities.

"Red's Old Lady has a name."

Jagger ignored that. "Last time there was an attempt at a negotiation, twenty-four ended up dead."

I made a little finger twirl, gesturing him to keep talking.

"And McQuestion's IT man says some of the communications can be traced to these coordinates."

Bloody damn. Jolene and Cupcake had slipped up somewhere. But it was too late to go back. "So you put two and two together and figured out Heather was an alias."

"And the woman you call Cupcake was Red's Old Lady in the Hells Angels."

"Not bad IT work. Hope you don't mind if we keep our weapons on you."

Jagger grinned and set his kickstand, but he stayed sitting, his jeans stretching over parts of him that I would not be interested in.

Not.

Never.

Liar.

"A fortified cabin, within a few miles of a major interstate highway, was in the hands of the MSA. Then in the hands of an OMW made-man. That would be you, Little Girl. And you gave that fortress away without McQuestion's consent. You *gave away property* to *Marconi*, a *Hells Angels chapter president*," he enunciated carefully, as if to point out my stupidity.

I chuckled and shrugged, a "so what?" expression on my face.

"Marconi then moved up in the Hells Angels. He's now a regional president, and he's so powerful he may as well be co-prez now. McQuestion is not happy."

Cupcake whispered into my earbud, "Damn. That's new intel. I should have known about it. Sorry, Shining. On the other hand, I did give McQuestion info about the other clubs."

"Uh-huh," I said to both of them.

Jagger shifted on his bike. "He wants to open negotiations with Little Girl early and explain to her what her future position will be in the organization." His tone told me how McQuestion expected this to go. He expected me to comply.

Once an OMW, always an OMW. Yeah. I knew the rules. I even lived by them. Mostly.

"Let's start out on the right foot here, Asshole. I won that property in *personal* combat and battle with *my* team against the Mara Salvatrucha Angels. My *gift* to *McQuestion* was to hand it over to a friendly, to keep that territory from falling back into the hands of the MSA. If McQuestion is smarter than your comments indicate so far, and takes advantage of my opening moves, he can initiate negotiations between Marconi and the national prez of the Hells Angels to stop the MSA for good. Or use the info to drive a wedge between the two. His choice. *I* gave him that opportunity with a small gift of *my* property, in the hopes that together we could stop the MSA from taking more territory and eventually moving on the OMW."

A hard expression claimed my face. "Only an idiot would think the MSA isn't going to go after the other clubs, the Boozefighters and the Black Sabbath too. McQuestion isn't—usually—an idiot. And the OMW received info from me. Intel about the MSA and the local HA chapter, and info

that some of the OMW members were working behind his
back with the Gov. and the military. Speaking of which, has
he rooted them out yet?"

Jagger's expression said he hadn't.

I snorted in derision. "*I* did that for the OMW. The
proper response from McQuestion is, 'Thank you, Little
Girl. Well done.' Not whatever the bloody damn hell this
shakedown is."

Jagger frowned, but there was a twinkle in his eyes.
"Marconi leveraged the fortress into a position of power.
Power imbalances always fall under the operational pur-
view of McQuestion."

I grunted and rubbed my lower face, whispering to
Cupcake, "He's right. I didn't think about that. I *hate* politics." Dropping my hand, I said, "Marconi is smart enough.
Proved that by not going to war against his own prez. You
trying to tell me McQuestion thinks the Old Man is smarter
than him?"

Jagger's grin went wider, exposing a crooked tooth on
the bottom row. I had insulted McQuestion, then hinted at
another insult, and then insulted some more. It wasn't quite
a challenge to his position, but I was getting awfully close.

Jagger said, "OMW wants something of equal value to
the fortress, in return for agreeing to attend the negotiations. He has suggestions."

"I'll bet he does. Tell him to talk to Cupcake, and if
what she offers doesn't make him happy, he can"—I hesitated, mentally apologizing to Pops for not being political
enough, and to Cupcake for probably making her job
harder—"he can bloody well piss off."

Jagger laughed. "Spoken like the daughter of Bill Smith."

I just stared. I was offering nothing that might tip the bal-
ance of power toward Marconi, Whip, or McQuestion. Not
until the parley when I could gauge the reactions of the men.

"McQuestion, Whip, and Marconi are in communication," he said, "and have agreed to the upcoming negotiations, which might actually come to something positive, as
each has had the other's kid as diplomatic hostages for the
last few weeks—Marconi's son, McQuestion's daughter—
and nobody's died. Yet. Whip finds the hostage exchange
amusing in a mediaeval structure sort of way."

I nodded. I had sorta facilitated that arrangement, but few knew that. "I'm still listening, Asshole."

"McQuestion wants Little Girl back in his organization."

Expecting that demand didn't stop my heart from falling.

If I complied, I'd eventually become the de facto leader, the McQuestion of the OMW, because I'd almost certainly make a mistake and infect the leaders of the OMW with my nanobots. I'd then have to live and breathe politics and war. *Ain't no way.* No emotion in my tone, I said, "After we cement all the negotiations and deal with the additional problems I'm bringing to the table, I'll discuss this with McQuestion. Not before."

"He wants the Simba."

"Everybody wants the Simba. They can try to take it. I'll feed their protein to the cats."

Spy let out a vicious sound I had heard before, a soft growl that meant *hunt and kill*. It was followed by a chorus of *"Kkkkk."*

Jagger's lips twitched, and then his eyes made a shift through emotions too fast to see and too fast for the nanobot connection between us to follow. He actually hesitated, as if he didn't want to say the next bit, and at the same time wanted to desperately. "He says to sweeten the deal you can have any available made-man you want in the organization."

Something low in my belly turned over. I went hot and liquid in all the right places. For all intents and purposes, McQuestion had just offered me Jagger. For my own. Just like women had been offered to made-men in the past. My nanobots began turning cartwheels. *Bloody sodding damn.*

"Clearly you are going deaf," I said. "*After* the negotiations, and what might come after that, in a time of peace and security, McQuestion and I can sit down and chat. Not until then. And I do *not* accept slaves. But as a gesture of goodwill, I'll tell you this for McQuestion: Whip and Marconi don't know it, but the Sabbath and Booze presidents are interested in attending the negotiations. I've extended an invitation to them too. Now go away."

Jagger's face fell as he computed the presence of other motorcycle-club presidents at a parley—the likelihood of ambush, fighting, death, and all-out war. To give him credit, his face eased into a smile and he laughed. Touched his bike on with a biomarker starter and did a tight U-turn. He puttered away.

I thought about that laugh—carefree, without rancor or sarcasm, truly amused. Thought about McQuestion's offer of a man to my taste, just as he offered a woman to a man. I grinned, wondering what would have happened if I'd wanted a woman of my own? Homosexuality was forbidden in the club, unless it was girl-on-girl stuff for an all-male audience. What if I'd gone against that proscription and flaunted it? Or, what if I'd just agreed and taken Jagger on the spot?

The heat in my belly rose another notch as the bike's muters faded into the distance. The cats turned and sauntered away.

"Assholes. Both of them." I swiveled around to see Cupcake and Amos standing in the shade of the office overhang.

There was nothing funny, but the two laughed.

Into my earbud, Cupcake said, "This negotiation is going to be. So. Much. Fun."

*
*

My clothes reeking like someone had died in them, I came in late from the junkyard and stifled a groan. The office had been transformed.

By her beaming, nervous expression, I knew that Cupcake had done all the . . . stuff. She had gone all-out on decorating, with sterling-silver utensils, fancy delicate china, and glasses with stems. A bottle of red wine, with a real cork, was sitting on the table. I hadn't known we had a bottle of wine and wondered if there were more stashed somewhere in the junkyard.

There were also cloth linens, a long narrow table she had probably found somewhere in the junkyard and placed along the command center, and serving trays filled with food. The command chair was missing. I had no idea where it had gone. I hadn't known it could be moved. Cupcake and I needed to have a chat.

After dinner. Which smelled fabulous.

In the fancy serving trays and some kind of big silver

dish with a flame underneath to keep food warm, was a feast. A huge salad from the expanded greenhouse was in a crystal bowl. A mixture of roasted herbed baby potatoes, beets, and fennel root was in one side of the flame-hot dish. Beside the pile of crispy roots was a roasted chicken. Someone—I was guessing Amos—had killed, cleaned, and plucked the bird. I hoped it was the crowing rooster that annoyed me to near death.

"Quick. Get cleaned up," Cupcake commanded. "And wash the grime from under your fingernails. What are you, some kind of heathen? I put a dress in the toilette compartment." She shooed me with her hands as if I was a flighty dog or something nasty. "Go on. We have company tonight."

I found myself in the personal toilette compartment, the door shut firmly behind me. I yelled through the door, "Did you manage Red this way?"

I made out a tinny voice yelling, "I managed *everyone* this way. Red woulda been prez if Warhammer hadn't come along."

"That's what scares me," I muttered. "That you'll figure out what I could do and be, that you'll take over and make it happen." And she'd do it in my name. Whether I wanted to be part of her plans or not. Yet, the fact that she was acting of her own free will was some small comfort and something I had wanted all along. It made her a . . . a free thrall.

Free thralls . . . *Bloody damn*. The idea that free thralls might want their queen elevated in status was scary. What if they thought the best way to serve me was to take over the world and they went about that without my input? *Bloody damn*.

Following the orders of my not-quite-a-thrall, I cleaned up and pulled on the dress Cupcake had hung on the door hook. It was a sort of an orange-gold shimmery thing and looked great on me. It also itched, but what the heck. The shoes were little strappy sandals. Pretty. God knew where she had found the outfit. She had also laid out makeup. I shoved it out of the way and gooped up my hair into spikes, wondering why I was doing this. And knowing it was to see Cupcake happy. That thought itched as bad as the stupid dress.

I opened the door and nearly tripped over my jaw. Mateo—out of his warbot suit—was sitting at the dinette. Except it wasn't really him. This Mateo had arms and legs and all of his head. He was also younger, had hair, and was wearing the dress blues of the CO of a starship. He wavered a bit, as if reality stuttered.

Mateo was an illusion. Or a laser representation. Or something else scientific I hadn't known Jolene could do.

"Mateo," I said carefully. "Cupcake. Amos."

"Forgive me if I don't stand," Mateo said, his mouth not moving and his voice coming through the speakers. "You look lovely, as always, Shining."

What the bloody hell?

"Yeah. Uh. You too. Well not lovely." I broke out into a sweat the instant the words left my mouth. "I mean, Cupcake looks lovely. Is it okay to tell a man he looks lovely?" In the super macho world of the OMW it would have gotten me backhanded and if conditions were wrong, could have gotten me killed.

"I'm not offended." I was fairly certain that there was laughter in Mateo's voice.

Cupcake was wearing black slacks and a black long-sleeved shirt and a white apron. Amos was wearing a freaking suit. And in through the door came Wanda and her shadow—what was their name? Alex? Yeah, Alex. And a dozen cats who rushed in, tails high. I glanced at the medbay to find it empty. Someone had released the neutered cats.

Wanda had cleaned up and dressed up, wearing a sheath dress and heels. I could associate this vision with my memory of her—clean, neat. Her demeanor was currently tentative but did nothing to hide the naturally capable and tough personality of the woman who had drawn a weapon on me the last day I saw her. She did however look a lot younger now that she was hydrated and fed. My nanobots had changed her.

When she saw me, her shoulders went back and her face took on a mulish expression.

Her kid stuck his—her—their?—head out from behind Wanda. Alex was dressed in jeans and a plaid shirt. I still had no idea of the kid's gender as the clothing and hair could have been either, but I figured I could get by without using pronouns for a while longer.

"Hey, Wanda," I said. "Hey, kid. Glad y'all could make it." That pretty much drained my party talk. "Um. Cupcake did all the work." Helplessly, I looked at Cupcake, who appeared oddly proud of me.

She gestured to one side of the dinette, across from not-Mateo. "We are so happy to have company and new nest mates. Please be seated." To me she added, "You sit there." She pointed next to Mateo's image, which chose that moment to waver in and out of focus.

"Damn it," Jolene said. "Hang on, Cap'n."

Nudged by Cupcake, I sat and hoped Mateo didn't reappear partially on top of me. I smothered nervous laughter and drank some clear stuff that turned out to be water. Mateo flickered into existence and smiled a wooden smile around at us. I glanced at his plate and shook my head. I knew in the depths of my mind that this was a dress rehearsal for Cupcake's vision of the future. Me as queen entertaining my nest.

Ghastly.

The rest of the evening was as unpleasant and nerve-wracking as the welcome. We made awkward small talk. We drank the bottle of really good wine and ate the excellent food. Cupcake had taken all sorts of Berger-chip lessons, and it was a fabulous meal. The cats sat and watched and accepted bits of chicken as their due, though I figured they were thinking that raw human would have been a better choice. They were on their best behavior, but they all had that predator look in their eyes.

When the plates were cleaned and everyone left, including most of the cats, I stripped and climbed into my bed. Tuffs and Spy joined me. I lay in the bed and stared at the ceiling for far too long, wondering what in the name of anything that might be holy was happening to my thralls.

*
*

I woke an hour before dawn, my thoughts moving, as always, to Harlan, who had been my best friend, the source of much of my intel in the junk business, and my only connection to the OMW. He'd been like a father to me until he was tortured and killed by Warhammer. Vengeance wasn't a god or a religion, but until I killed Harlan's murderer, the destruction of Warhammer and her nest would be the center vision of my life. Like every other morning when I first woke, I pledged to kill her for him. If that made killing her my God, then I was surely going to hell.

I rolled over, dislodging Spy, who was draped over my head on my pillow. The command chair was back in place.

I needed to have a long chat with my . . . whatever Cupcake was to me.

My feet hit the floor; my fist hit the coffee maker on. I let the two cats out, cracked their outdoor water bowls free of ice, and started my day. Same as always. But today wasn't the same as always. Today was the negotiation with the biker clubs, and I had no idea who might show up to talk—or who might show up to kill.

Mateo said into the office speaker system, "Heading out, Shining. Full camo, and all defensive measures active. The Simba and I will be in place when you arrive, if intervention or exfil is needed."

If he wasn't needed, no one would ever see him. If he was needed, the shit would likely have hit the fan and blood would have already been spilled.

"Be careful," I said to him. He didn't reply.

*
*

The negotiations were to be held at Marconi's fortress, the one I gave to him in McQuestion's name—which, in hindsight, hadn't necessarily been smart. It wouldn't be an easy drive, not with the bandits, gangs, and poor road conditions, but we could manage.

As Cupcake and I swung into the old truck, which Mateo and Cupcake had loaded and argued over, I figured we had about a twenty percent chance of getting away alive and about a two percent chance of getting away without spilled blood. I also figured we had about a one percent chance we would get there and back without someone trying to make off with Cupcake's negotiation goodies.

Spy's clowder jumped inside too, this time with Tuffs and Notch in charge, sitting on the dash. Spy landed in my

lap instead of on the dash with her queen. The presence of
Tuffs and Notch bothered me on some level, but nothing
was clear about why I should be worried, so I let it slide.

In the back of the flatbed, Amos positioned himself in
his recliner, which he had rescued on our last jaunt, weapons across his lap. Wanda and Alex were beside him, curled
up on a daybed they had found somewhere. I didn't want
to leave them in the junkyard unsupervised, and they had a
day or so before they transitioned to my new nanobots, so
they could travel. And for this trip there was a nice sun-
shade over the passengers in the flatbed, a retractable
awning taken from the RV where my dinette set and small
fridge had come from. The rigging had all the earmarks of a
shade-tree mechanic, meaning it was ugly but it worked.

I caught a glimpse of other cats leaping high into the
back of the truck.

"Tuffs? Why so many cats?" I asked.

She turned her greener-than-green eyes to me and
blinked before turning back to peer out the windshield.

I had not planned on the cats. With the odds of making this work so low—getting the leaders to agree on anything at all, rescuing Evelyn, killing Warhammer, and living
through it without infecting everyone I came into contact
with—I should have been worried at this last-minute ad-
dition. But fighting the cats sounded like a war I couldn't
win. When Cupcake turned the key and the ancient truck
began to rumble, my worries began to lift.

"I'm puttin' on that singer I like," Jolene said over the
speakers. Her favorite song began to play, and it was like a
blessing. *Jolene, Jolene, Jolene, Joleeeen.* Unfortunately,
Cupcake joined in, and while my nanobots had given her
youth and excellent health, they had not given her a voice
at all. She still sounded like cats screaming. Tuffs's ear tabs
folded in, and she turned a regal head to stare at Cupcake
in disdain. Spy buried her head in my armpit. I laughed, the
sound unexpected and carefree. If I was feeling even the
slightest bit positive, it was because of the presence of my
nest. I needed them as much as they needed me.

I tapped my tiny earbud and said, "Jolene, the helm is
yours. Take care of the place while we're gone."

"Shining Sugah, I got it." As Cupcake pulled us down

the drive, Jolene added, "Full alert. Shields active, RVACs in flight, all weapons are a go. Automatic defensive systems active. Hey Gomez, you ever heard of phone sex?"

I tapped my mic and shut my earbuds off. Jolene's relationship with Gomez—the Bug ship's AI—was not something I wanted to know about. I checked the truck's weapons systems, sensors, and integrated screens, which had been seriously upgraded using the military equipment I had confiscated from Morrison's. I had set fire to the place, leaving his body to burn.

Killing Morrison had been step one in getting revenge for Harlan's death.

Uniting the motorcycle clubs was step two.

Destroying Warhammer and her nest was step three.

And I'd succeed or die trying.

*

*

We were a few klicks from the armored house, and three-quarters of the way to busted spines and concussions from the bouncing of the old truck, when Jolene silenced the music and said, "Mateo is in position and has reported. An armored Harley One Rider pulled into the parking area. Make of bike and body size and weight of its rider appear to match that of Logan Jagger."

All sorts of things went through my mind, all of them good, none of them helpful. "Patch Mateo's screens through," I requested.

"Copy that, Sugah. Audio to follow, though the distance is problematic. CO Mateo was unable to position an audio spike closer than six meters to the fortification."

On the screen, now integrated into the truck's armored plaz-silk windshield, a view opened. It was Jagger, sitting on his bike, his position much like the one he had when talking to me in my driveway, except now he was wearing his fully patched OMW kutte over a full set of Dragon Scale military armor and was loaded down with weapons I hadn't known he had. He looked like a man who had gone to war and come home with his enemies' booty. He sat on his bike, helmetless, his warboots planted in the dirt. There was a white flag tied to his handlebar.

Marconi stepped out of the front door of his stronghold—alone, unweaponed, and wearing jeans and a dress shirt. To his side a girl appeared, fully weaponed, tall but very slender. I had never seen her in person, but recognized her from the photos Jolene had obtained from deep data searches.

Camilla Mary Gamble, McQuestion's daughter, had nearly white hair and eyes like icebergs. Her skin was so white it appeared translucent, odd skin in this post-WIMP-bomb world, where the Earth had little shielding from the sun's radiation and pale-skinned people usually died young from melanoma.

Audio came over the speakers, tinny and distant. "Where's Jacopo?" Marconi asked.

"Behind me, bringing up the gear." Toneless. Offering nothing. "He's driving a truck loaded with chairs, a tented covering, and a table." Jagger grunted with a sound that was probably supposed to be laughter. "McQuestion owns a round table. Like Arthur's. And your kid appropriated it for the meeting."

"Jacopo?" Marconi sounded disbelieving.

"Yeah. He was put in charge of meeting prep. He's a good kid. Smart."

Instead of responding to the compliment, Marconi said, "I have two and a half kilos of roasted coffee beans, ready to be ground."

Jagger scraped his feet against the dirt. "Coffee's good. McQuestion has an unopened bottle of fifty-year-old tequila he thinks might be good too. For toasting a safe and successful negotiation." The wind caught the white flag and it twirled.

Marconi nodded, then pursed his lips thoughtfully. "I hear we got more coming, and somebody's bringing a smoked wild sow and some piglets."

"That would be the Booze. Sabbath's Old Lady is a baker. So we got bread coming. And a couple cakes."

"I got a grill already hot. Commercial fryer," Marconi said, and I realized they were trying to outdo each other. "And a load of potatoes. And salt and pepper. Makings of a feast, even if it will never be as good as my Italian."

"Best Italian I ever tasted. Even in Italy."

Marconi nodded and turned his head to the side. "Talk first. Eat after."

"Agreed. McQuestion will honor parley rules."

"Marconi and Charles Whip will honor parley rules. But will the others?"

"We'll have to see," Jagger nearly growled out. "If not, the battle will be fun. Figuring out who is on whose side will be even more fun."

"It always is," Marconi agreed.

On my screen, a low-sided truck, an ancient diesel even older than mine, rolled into the parking area. Jacopo turned it off and leaped out of the driver's door, lithe and manly. He landed and looked to the front porch. Something changed in his body language. Not something I could identify from this angle, but something strong, like a punch to the gut. He nodded to his father and went to work unloading the truck.

"I'm leaving three men to help your son," Jagger said. "He's in charge of the set-up. He will not be visiting his family until after the negotiations are concluded."

"His mother will not be happy with that arrangement, but I accept, nonetheless. Camilla will not visit her family until the same time frame."

"Understood," Jagger said.

Jacopo bent forward from the waist in a small bow to his father, and then again to Jagger. "I honor my word and my father's vow."

Camilla bowed too, her white hair falling across her white face. "I honor the decisions made here and now."

"Checking perimeters," Jagger said.

His engine came to life, sounding like a dragon from old myths, and Jagger motored away from the house.

"I do believe that Jagger is heading your way, Shining," Mateo said, and there might have been amusement or maybe boredom in his tone. It was hard to tell. "Give him a hug from me," he added. Yeah. Amusement.

"That tree you pushed off the road the last time we came this way," I said to Cupcake, "is just ahead."

"I'll pull over there and we can eat a quick snack," she said, "and check ammo. You can take a walk. Talk privately."

"That works."

*

*

The sound of the Harley came to me, bounding off the low

hills. I was standing in the middle of the road, just past where Cupcake had squished a dead man with the truck on our last trip this way. I was unarmed except for a blaster strapped to my thigh, and as the rumble of the bike approached around the next bend, I uncrossed my arms and put my fists on my hips, waiting, legs spread, feet planted, riding boots steady on the cracked asphalt.

Jagger came around the bend, and I knew the moment he saw me. That awareness was like being stabbed straight into the solar plexus. I missed my next breath, pressure in my chest. He slowed, and the bike came to a stop. The motor died.

This time he got off the bike and stared into the sun's glare through sunglasses he hadn't worn at Marconi's fortress. He hooked his thumbs into blade sheaths in his armor. It was the same kind of Dragon Scale armor we had taken from Morrison's, the same kind I had brought to barter. Looked as if he'd taken the suit he wore when we fought together last. I hadn't asked. I hadn't given it to him. Jagger was the kind of man who took what he wanted. Best I remembered that.

But . . . I wished I had been able to see Marconi's face up close when he caught sight of Jagger wearing the military's best and latest gear. I bet he nearly pissed his britches.

"Asshole," I said by way of greeting.

"Little Girl. I got some things to say. Things McQuestion hasn't sanctioned."

Hasn't sanctioned. Not *wouldn't* sanction. Meaning McQuestion *might* sanction? Might *intend* to sanction? Had maybe given a nod and a wink at a private agreement to something that might someday become public? There were a lot of loopholes in that, but I tilted my head in agreement.

"Your wire off?"

Jagger nodded once, a disgruntled expression on his face. He had resented the wire and the questioning of his loyalty. Being an Enforcer was power, status, and honor. Being mine had threatened his world and his position in it.

"Then I'm listening."

He pulled off his sunglasses so I could see his chocolate-brown eyes. I shoved my orange lenses up onto my head, revealing my orange eyes. Some things needed to be face-to-face, literally.

"I want you," Jagger said. "And I don't think it's the nanobots. Not anymore."

I wanted him too, but there were a lot of problems with that scenario. Always had been. First and foremost was that Jagger belonged to McQuestion. Even if McQuestion gave Jagger to me, he would intend his gift to watch me, eyes and ears on everything I did, and report back. Probably even bedroom talk and bedroom acts.

But I remembered Jagger's arms around me, demanding, his mouth plundering, remembered his taste, his scent. He was a big man, both physically and in that thing called *presence*: part charisma, part machismo, part brains, all powerful, capable, violent, and smart. I liked smart. I'd have liked Jagger even without the nanos binding us together. But the silence had stretched too long.

"You want me," I said. "Sex."

"More than sex. Way more. That said, I promise you it would be"—he slowed his words—"mind-blowing. Screaming. Hot. Sweaty. Sex." His words were like melted chocolate dripped from a big spoon.

It took a few heartbeats before I could find a breath and respond. "I'm not someone you just"—I mentally apologized to Pops—"fuck."

He blinked at the crudity, knowing I never used that word. His eyes widened and something passed through them, too fast to read. "That's not—"

"I'm Little Girl," I interrupted. "A made-man. I'm worth more than a turn in the sheets. And I don't want a man given to me by someone else." If Jagger and I had a chance at anything, and that didn't look likely, he needed to see me for everything that I was. He needed to be able to get mad at me. Argue and fight back with me. Spar with me and not worry that he might hurt his queen. "I don't want a slave in my bed."

Jagger turned red. That was a good start, so I pushed it a bit more. "And I want a man who wants me for me, not because of nanobots turning his brain to mush, or because his boss said to woo me, screw me, and report back." I dropped my arms and let one hand dangle near my blaster.

"For now, I've got a parley and then, hopefully, I'll be putting together a crew to go after Warhammer. When she's done, maybe I'll call you."

"You'll call—? And what am I supposed to do until then?" Jagger ground out.

He had clearly never been told by a woman that she'd be the one to call.

I chuckled. "Your job. The job of a national enforcer. Arrange safe transport for the leaders, I assume. And then, if McQuestion agrees to assist, help plan and carry out the attack on Warhammer's nest. Just do your job, Asshole." I started to turn away and tilted my head as if I'd just thought of something. "Oh. Cupcake found some jewelry you might like. I'll make sure she brings you the stash, and you can pick out some pretties for yourself."

"Pick out jewel— You're . . ." He stopped. Jagger was not used to being treated like a woman usually was in the OMW. "You can't lie to me. You want me."

"Why? Because you're so good in the sack?"

He blinked.

I walked away, calling over my shoulder, "You look pretty today, Asshole."

I approached the truck to see Cupcake standing in the middle of the road with our cohorts, three sets of armor in boxes and a donning station in a huge wooden case sitting in the middle of the road behind them. She said, "You told him to go away, didn't you?"

I scowled. Was I so easy to read?

"Damn it, Shining. You want him. He wants you. You need a nest. What is wrong with you?"

Wishing I had an answer, I said, "Let's get this done."

"You need to freshen up, put on some lipstick, and do something with that hair. You didn't even comb it when you got out of bed today, did you?"

I shrugged. I was fairly certain I had a comb. Somewhere.

Cupcake frowned at me and blew out a resigned breath. "Amos and Wanda and me need to armor up as your security detail. Might as well do it here."

Without answering, I swung into the cab, spotting a meal on the minuscule table. Just the sight of it turned my stomach fast, suggesting that I was nervous or something. I ignored it and went to the tiny toilette behind the two seats. On the bunk were fresh clothes and a device as long as my opened hand, shaped like an old electric shaver. There was a tiny hemp-paper note stuck on it that said, *"Here's your new toy. Turn it on. Press the rounded end to a person's skin and push the button, and it will measure the presence and amount of nanobots in the person's system. Try it."*

I followed directions, and a tiny light glowed green until I shoved the rounded end against my own skin. Then the light turned red and the little dial flipped from 0 to100. Yeah. I had nanos. Big surprise.

When I left the sleeping cab, I sat to eat, forcing myself to down the salad, the vegetable protein, and some leftover roasted veggies. I drank reheated chicken stock Cupcake had made from the bones of the chicken at the fancy dinner. It was hard to get sufficient protein these days, and the stock was not only delicious, it settled my stomach. There was coffee in an insulated mug. So good.

An hour after I entered, I emerged, full of lunch and wearing fresh jeans; a clean shirt with the sleeves rolled up; a necklace with a religious medal for luck; un-stinky clean socks inside my worn, scraped, dusty boots; leather armbands I hadn't worn in years; and black biker's gloves with pointed steel knuckle rivets where they'd do the most damage if I had to hit someone. The nano detector was in a small sheath on my left leg. I was wearing orange lipstick to match my orange sunglasses. I figured I looked okay, though I had only a small mirror to see myself.

I swung down from the cab. The first thing I saw was my security detail wearing Dragon Scale armor in matching camo patterns. Then I spotted the matte black Harley parked beside the big rig.

My Harley.

I hadn't laid eyes on her since the day I took over Smith's. She had been in storage. Hadn't been cranked. Hadn't been touched in years. Someone had done some work on her.

If her name on the gas tank hadn't still been prominent, I might not have recognized her. I'd called her

Death's Reaper, after the collector of souls, and her name had been painted in electric blue with a death sickle across the bottom of the name.

Something like joy flooded through me at the sight of her. Walking slowly, I took my bike in.

She was a wartime bike, a Harley Machinegun, a limited edition produced only for a few years. Bikes built for military applications now were larger, meaner, like Jagger's One Rider. This Harley had been built for a much smaller me, with sleek lines for speed, camouflage, basic shielding, and minimal weapons. Well, several small weapons and one big-assed weapon. It had been built to hold a mounted M249 Para Gen VI, a magazine-fed machine gun with extended mags, a weapon similar to the one at the junkyard, but newer, fancier, built for fighting the PRC in the war. Currently, the Para Gen was not mounted on the bike. Probably a good thing at a negotiation.

Hubris, maybe, but my Reaper was still the prettiest thing I'd ever laid eyes on. And even with all the changes, she still looked like me. Someone had rebuilt her for my longer legs, chopped her a bit to add size and impact. And her shielding and camo patterns had been updated. There was a shotgun, along with a nine-millimeter and a brand-new military blaster in a multipurpose weapons sheath built into the bike's frame.

I shook my head and let a smile cross my face. I met Cupcake's blue eyes and said, "She's gorgeous. Your work?"

Cupcake made a small *harrumphing* sound. "Berger chips aren't good enough for most of this work. I rebuilt the engine. *That* I could learn. The bodywork is Amos all the way."

I looked at the big guy who had willingly joined my nest just for the possibility of being with Cupcake. "Nice work, both of you. I'm impressed."

Wanda was standing nearby. Her kid was hiding behind her back with only their head facing the bike. "Ms. Shining," Alex said, "that sure is pretty. Can I ride it?"

"Not this time," I said. "But maybe someday." To their mother, I added, "You look good in the armor. Dangerous. Follow Amos's or Cupcake's lead. Don't shoot anybody. Keep your kid safe, preferably in the truck." I looked at Alex. "You hear gunfire or see a fight start, you get in the cab and lock the doors until I tell you different. It'll be scary, but you'll be safe and I won't waste time worrying about you."

"I can shoot a gun. If somebody would give me one," Alex said with a fierce expression.

"No." I felt my command secure itself onto the kid's nanos. For a good two seconds I hated myself and the fact that I had unwittingly made a thrall of a child. "Not today. Unless your mother says otherwise, your job is to keep the truck doors locked so we can get away, and keep yourself safe. Period."

Alex heaved a dramatic sigh that made me think *girl*, and their mother heaved a similar sigh, but of relief.

I straddled Reaper and pressed the start button. She purred to life, her engine reverberating through my body and right into my soul. I started to turn her, when Cupcake displayed my old, and far too small, OMW kutte across the seat behind me so it could be seen. My eyes filled with tears. *Bloody damn*. This felt good.

I pulled away as the cats, who had been everywhere underfoot, jumped back into the cab and the flatbed, and the rest of my nest hopped inside too. With Death's Reaper rumbling beneath me, I motored down the road to the fortress where possibilities, both good and bad, awaited me.

It was time for my grand entrance.

*

*

Aware of the big truck behind me, I pulled slowly down the drive to the fortified mansion I had given to Marconi—after I shot it to hell and back and killed most of the men inside.

In front of the repaired, fortified log house—once again armored and weaponed for war—was a broken concrete drive and parking area. The mega-gun that was once visible through a gunport was now hidden behind a pretty stained-glass window which was totally out of place on the fortified walls. The red glass roses below the HA's skull-and-wings emblem stood out like a threat. I wasn't certain the weapon had been repaired or replaced after our attack here not so long ago, but if so, it was a clear advantage to Marconi.

Yeah. I got why McQuestion was pissed that I gave

away the cabin fortress.

In the center of the parking area, an open-air tent had been erected with a round table beneath it. There were six chairs, all but one with a man sitting in it. Cigars in their mouths. Liquor in shot glasses, even this early in the day. Five important leaders from the largest motorcycle clubs in the country. In the world.

I had never seen OMW and Hells Angels talking. There had been parleys in the past, but most had resulted in bloodshed and the Hand of the Law showing up. This was new and dangerous. Especially so because the vice president and warlord, McQuestion himself, was on-site instead of the talking-head prez of the OMW.

In the OMW, the so-called prez was a PR specialist. The real power was the second-in-command—the VP, the warlord, always referred to as McQuestion to keep his identity secret. But the VP, Roy Gamble himself, was up front and not hiding. And Marconi was sitting next to Charles Whip, prez of the HA, showing just how much power Marconi now had as a regional prez. Definitely number two in the organization. Besides the people I recognized, there was a fully patched made-man of the Boozefighters and a made-man of the Black Sabbath, sitting to either side of the Hells Angels' contingent.

HA, Sabbath, Booze, and OMW. Black bikers sitting with white bikers at the same round table, all unarmed. Something mythologic about that. Or not. My stomach roiled, and I thought I might hurl, but I held it in.

There were motorcycles parked in groups everywhere. War bikes, pre-war bikes, chopped bikes, some crotch rockets built for speed, and groups of people, all segregated by organization, race, and gender. That segregation would never do.

Not joining any group, I pulled my bike at an angle so they could all get a good look at me, and powered down. Behind me, the big rig eased in, the jake brakes sending a juddering reverberation through the front parking area. Through my orange glasses, I studied the men at the table.

I hadn't seen McQuestion since my father's funeral, a decade ago. Roy looked good—fit, still red haired. Charles Whip was the current national HA president stationed in

Durham, North Carolina, and former chapter prez out of Berdoo Charter in San Bernadino, California. Back before the PRC landed and the Mara Salvatrucha began their hostile takeover of the Hells Angels, Berdoo was the most prestigious house in the HA.

Last Harlan told me, there were twenty or twenty-five chapter houses left, the rest having been taken over by the MSA. What remained of Whip's organization would soon be taken over by Warhammer; he just hadn't admitted he was losing yet. Whip needed all the numbers he could get, which had to be the reason he had promoted Marconi. Probably gave him control over several chapter houses and territory beyond Charleston.

Mateo said into my earbud, "The Booze is Henry Thibodaux, out of New Orleans. He has to be a new prez. The Sabbath is J'Ron Walker, out of Old New York. Also a new prez but Cupcake uncovered his story. He shot his way to the top and was voted in as prez unanimously. Both are augmented, toes to teeth. In a fight, they'll rip your arms off with their bare hands. You're walking on eggshells here, Shining."

Walking on eggshells? More like walking on eggs filled with TNT.

Each organization's made-men were standing in well-defined camps behind them, armed of course. Most wore war patches, showing that they were warriors seasoned during WWIII. None of them was drinking. Their Old Ladies and any female made-men were relaxing behind the muscle, near the bikes, also separated into groups.

Behind Marconi's chair stood three of his children: his psychopath daughter—and not-so-secret weapon—Mina; and two of his sons, Lorenzo and Enrico, who, by the longing look he sent me, was still my thrall, though not desperate enough to cross club lines and come to me. Interesting. A strong authority figure was keeping Enrico where he belonged, with his family. McQuestion's daughter, Camilla, was standing with them, but as far as possible from Mina. Something in her body language suggested that the time she'd been forced to be with Marconi's bunch had been difficult.

Jagger was standing at point behind McQuestion, and

he glanced my way out of the corner of his eye. He had the best shooting vantage, but his fancy new armor would also take the first hit if shots were fired. And he hadn't engaged his helmet, making a head shot a sniper's only choice. Marconi's son Jacopo, the hostage in McQuestion's camp, stood with Jagger and the OMWs, facing his father and family.

The Booze and the Sabbath were watching me behind sunglasses. Evaluating the person who had assigned Cupcake the job of calling and arranging this little meeting.

Marconi lifted his shot glass and sipped. McQuestion kept his back to me, probably thinking he was putting me in my place. Everything said and done here would have multiple purposes and meanings. I'd need video to study later. Softly, I murmured, "You getting this?"

Jolene said, "Sure 'nuff. Multiple angles because I hacked into Marconi's and McQuestion's security cams."

I chuckled. The sound of my laughter finally made McQuestion turn around and look at me, which felt like a win. But I had no idea what to do now that I had made my grand entrance.

The cats exploded out of the truck cab and leaped from the flatbed in clowders of three or five or seven. They scattered silently, racing under cars or into the fractal shadows of bikes. No one seemed to notice them. Yet, all the cats turned toward me; all the cat eyes were on me. Waiting.

I fought a shiver and dismounted my bike. Wanda stood behind, covering my six. I spotted Cupcake and Amos, who had maneuvered fast, standing under the tent, behind the empty chair at the round table. Them standing there was an emotional gut-punch.

In my deepest heart, I had expected one of two possibilities: to address the group while standing to one side, as befitted my gender, to give them my intel, lay out my suggestions, and then be sent away like a child while the boys talked; or to have to fight my way to even being listened to. But Cupcake had always had higher aspirations. Now I had a strange feeling that her plans had come to fruition, and the chair was mine. That McQuestion was allowing me, a female made-man, to sit at the table with him.

This was . . . interesting. To my knowledge, it was unprecedented. And it was definitely dangerous.

Which Cupcake had to know. Yet, her eyes were wide with excitement, and she made the tiniest of movements toward the chair as Amos pulled it out. The two were like some kind of romantic bodyguards—both of them weaponed up and wearing the same model armor that Jagger wore. All this could be sending a message that I was aligned with the OMW. Which I was, by vows and spilled blood. My place at the table made me number two in the OMW . . . or it made me something else entirely. Perhaps a traitor, someone who had walked away from the club and the vows that bound me—an enemy, if McQuestion chose to see it that way. This kind of ambiguity was perilous to my staying alive.

I tossed the too-small kutte over my shoulder to indicate I wasn't an enemy to the OMW, but wasn't siding with them either. I walked languidly, as if bored, to the tent, my boots crunching gravel in the oddly silent clearing. Walked into the shade. And stopped beside the empty seat. When I was a kid, there had been few parleys of biker clubs and none I had actually attended because of the potential for violence. There had also been no female made-men then. I didn't know the current protocol for a meeting like this, but Old Ladies didn't sit unless asked to.

However, I wasn't an Old Lady; I was Little Girl. Rules didn't apply to me. I probably wasn't supposed to speak either, but Cupcake and I had discussed early on that I had to talk with confidence, had to draw the lines, establish my position.

So I sat, and when a shot glass was put into my hand, I sipped.

Holy mama. Excellent tequila. It went down smooth.

Cupcake said, "Shining Smith. One of the few who came back alive after putting a nuke into a Mama-Bot. The only one of the Mama-Bot raiders still alive today. One of the first female made-men of the OMW. War hero, survivor, and the made-man who could have been owner of all you see around you, this fortification, by right of . . . military acquisition. Instead, in an act of good will, in hopes for this meeting today, to keep it from falling back into MSA hands, and in thanks for the help of the Hells Angels chapter prez of Charleston, West Virginia, when she took this house from Rico "Three Fingers" Garcia Perez, top man of the MSA, she gave it to Old Man Marconi."

The men around the table stared at me, looking me over. Their regard was heavy as a lead blanket.

"She's willing to offer something of value to McQuestion and to the Boozefighters and the Black Sabbath. So. You all know this, but Shining is here to broker a temporary peace, and assistance in the war on a mutual enemy. If the men and women gathered here are not interested in going to war against the MSA, the road out is that way." She pointed at the drive. The men glanced over, then returned their collective gazes to me.

Everything had a purpose, I reminded myself. And a cost.

"Gentlemen," I said.

"Little Girl," McQuestion said. "Why aren't you wearing your kutte?"

Amos took my kutte and draped it over the back of my chair. I breathed in the tequila fumes to settle my stomach, sipping instead of shooting the fine liquor, making them wait. It was probably bad form to puke on the VIPs. I almost grinned but the issue of not wearing a kutte was important. Men and their fashion choices . . .

"Doesn't fit," I said. "And I don't sew. When Pops died, I was thirteen. I grew into an adult, and when the kutte no longer fit, I took it off." I stared hard at McQuestion. "But I never gave up the vows." My tone said, *Once an Outlaw, always an Outlaw, but don't push it*.

He tilted his head, his expression saying that nothing was over, and that there would be a return to my position in the OMW. I didn't smile. I wasn't a *thing* to be traded. *I* was Little Girl. That didn't stop my stomach from roiling with tension, but I didn't have to let my nerves show.

"McQuestion. Whip. Marconi. Gentlemen." I gave a small nod to the men I'd never met.

"Bengal," the Boozefighter said. "Prez."

"Mama-Killer," the Black Sabbath said. When my eyebrows went up, he added, "I helped nuke a Mama-Bot in Mobile."

"Inside?" I asked.

"Heeelll no." His tone said he wasn't that dumb. "I set a small nuke on the treads. The kid who went inside never came back out."

Bloody hell. "Pleasure," I said.

Marconi said, "We have all been appropriately informed about the woman with the MSA, Clarisse Warhammer, the woman who poisoned my son."

I nodded. I swallowed back stomach acid. Watched the made-men watch each other and me. They ignored Cupcake and Amos. Big mistake, that.

"We also wish to provide information," Marconi said, hands spread in a magnanimous gesture, "free of charge, and outside the purview of this meeting. The president of the MSA is said to have been deposed and is on the move."

That was a polite phrase for "running for cover." Marconi sipped his very good tequila, his black eyes watching the others.

"This Warhammer has not yet been voted in as president, and word from an informant suggests she has divided the club. But she is living in Garcia Perez's main fortress. She has taken over his people. For all intents and purposes, Warhammer is now number one in the MS Angels, and with her poison and her ability to force compliance, she does not need a vote. It is simply hers for the taking."

I sipped some more. *Really good tequila.* "I'm aware she took over the bunker at the intersection of old I-77 and I-81, near Fort Chiswell," I said. That indicated I already knew all about the bunker and that I had been offered nothing by Marconi.

Spy leaped to the table and deposited a huge dead rat in the center before she jumped down. I couldn't help it. I burst out laughing. No one joined me. Amos leaned over, picked up the oversized rat by the tail, and tossed it under a car. It had to weigh more than Spy.

McQuestion's eyes had followed the cat, finally noticing all the cats everywhere. His gaze tracked to me.

"She was offering a tithe," I said, "while proving she's a hunter, a killer, and strong."

"Warhammer," Marconi said, bringing us back to the negotiation table. "The poison she uses to take over people's minds lasts seventy-two hours outside of her body, yes?"

"Yes," I said. Cupcake rested her hand on my shoulder as she leaned past me to pour more tequila for everyone. I didn't acknowledge her kindness, because important people in a biker club treated all such actions as their due. I sipped the tequila, and my stomach began to settle. Or maybe it was simply Cupcake's touch. *I could do this*. Cupcake stepped back.

"You can cure the people she infects?" McQuestion asked me.

"To date, with the med-bay protocols I've devised, I'm at seventy-five percent survival rate. All the success stories were the recent ones." I shrugged when Marconi glared at me. He hadn't asked about survival rates when I healed his son. I hadn't volunteered.

"We all know where she is," McQuestion said. "Why should we need your help taking her out? Why should any of us risk working together on your word and your intel, when you walked away from your own people?" His face hardened when he said, softly and slowly, "No loyalty."

Not having loyalty was often a death sentence.

No one shot me. That made this a real question, not an accusation.

I sipped, thinking. I still needed him, his intel, and his firepower. Which meant I had to give him something as important as the fortress I gave to Marconi. The Boozefighter and the Black Sabbath would want something too. Information was often as important as land and trade goods. I shrugged slightly and let a small smile onto my face. "*We* know where in the bunker she sleeps. Where her people sleep. We know where her armaments are located. We know where the power source is. Where her food is. We have schematics and floorplans of the entire bunker."

No one responded.

I lifted a hand, one finger pointing at Cupcake. "You all know Red's Old Lady. She was taken over by Warhammer's poison and forced to work with her. It's like Stockholm Syndrome and brainwashing, but more. It's a lot like being possessed. She and Red had no choice except to obey her. But Cupcake wanted out. When Red was killed trying to take me over, she came to me. My protocols brought her back to herself. I can save any of your people who get taken over by Warhammer."

Before he could talk more about loyalty and vows, I turned my orange sunglasses to Charles Whip, on the other side of Marconi. "Your organization was in danger. Cupcake didn't want to risk going to an HA chapter in case it fell too. And with the speed Warhammer has taken over your territory, it looks as though she made a wise decision." It was a slap. It said he was weak. His eyes went hard and cold. "You want to bargain?" I said before he could reply or challenge me. "Then bargain for the death of Warhammer and help take back your chapters from the MSA. That's it. That's what you get from me. My help to destroy Warhammer and the MSA. You get back your land, your chapter houses, the spoils, the people."

I looked at the Booze and the Sabbath. "You two can wipe the amusement off your faces. You need weapons. You've already joined forces in a loose confederation because your territories are under slow attack by PRC bots."

The self-titled Bengal of the Black Sabbath blinked. Mama-Killer's face went harder. They were pissed off that I knew their weakness. *Tough.*

"Word is you got second-gen Perkers invading," I said. "Some say they're a smaller version of Mama-Bots. Killing a Mama-Bot will be a lot harder this time. I'm sure the PRC AIs learned from the end of the war how to kill better. Faster. Probably the newer, smaller models will have no access from the outside, even for small bodies. No way to get a nuke in. And most people aren't willing to sacrifice their children to get inside one."

Like I had been. My own father had put me in major harm's way to kill a Mama-Bot. I sipped my tequila, not letting them see my reaction to my own words.

"I have . . . let's call them *trade goods*, that will make your fight against the bots easier, even without official military support." That meant I had military weapons. I waited until they looked at Amos and Cupcake, all decked out for war.

"Where'd you get military weapons?" Bengal asked.

I grinned enough to show teeth. "My supplier told me they fell off a truck. More important, I know how to destroy nanobots inside a Mama-Bot."

Their faces, so good at poker and bargaining and killing, went still and cold. "You lie," Bengal said.

"Nope. Even the military doesn't know how." I let the small smile widen. "I'll share the tech and the methodology with you."

Mateo hissed into comms, "You'd give that away?"

"In return for all that, all my help, my tech, I want two things: a prisoner being held in Warhammer's bunker. One person. And then I want Warhammer dead. That's it. The rest of the shit is yours."

This time there was no reaction. But I knew what they were thinking. If they had intel and tech the military didn't have, they didn't need the military at all. They could cancel all the semisecret military contracts that kept them bound. They could take over.

It was working. I could see it in their nonexpressions. I took a breath, caught a scent, and my skin suddenly . . . *itched* wasn't the right word. More like my nerves crawled, my senses felt something toxic on the breeze. Something—some*one*—only another queen would recognize.

I raised my glass at Cupcake and said, "Your turn."

Without missing a beat, Cupcake took over the negotiations. She had done enough research to know exactly what trade goods each person at the table wanted, needed, and would agree to.

I needed to watch the crowd. That whiff-sensation was the presence of enemy nanobots. It made sense. There was no way that this meeting and the reason for it hadn't made its way through the biker community and eventually to Warhammer's nest. The crawly smell-sensation told me that she had found access to members of the clubs. *My enemy had thralls here.* I needed to stop them from hearing the negotiations, stop them from leaving and reporting back to her.

How many? Where? What were their orders? My heart rate soared.

Cupcake offered her wares. Amos lifted trade items out of the flatbed for everyone's perusal. The VIPs sent their quartermasters, armorers, and weapons masters to examine the trade goods while they sat, chatted, and drank, trying to show how important they themselves were and how unimportant my offerings were. I sat with them, silent, waiting, watching.

Just about the time their people started hard negotiations, there was movement in the crowd: three made-men from three different clubs walked slowly to the back of my truck and stood together. One was a Black Sabbath, his skin glistening with fever sweat in the mild weather. He looked as if he had been newly transitioned—flop sweat, a case of the shakes. The second man belonged to Whip—white guy, grizzled, a beer belly that hung over his riding leathers, his gray beard in multiple braids. The third was a woman—tough, hard as nails, clearly former military. I recognized her from long ago. If Harlan's last info had been up to date, she was McQuestion's number-two enforcer, who reported directly to Jagger. Razor McBride. Her head swiveled to me. There was a semiautomatic weapon on her right side, violence in her eyes, and a promise of blood in her body language.

With the nano detector, I could prove that the three had nanobots in their bloodstreams, hopefully without revealing that I was a nanobot queen myself. But I needed to get close enough to smell their sweat to determine for certain what kind of nanobots had taken them over—Warhammer's or PRC nanobots. Either was a danger.

I set my tequila aside and started to push away from the table.

Left-handed, Razor pulled a blade and wiped it across her thigh, letting the sun glint across the steel. She wanted to fight me. I could feel that desire through the air between us. I wanted to fight her too, or my nanobots did. She *had* to be Warhammer's.

Warhammer had gotten her claws in deep. How many more were there? And were they about to start shooting?

Razor flashed the blade at me. Beside her, the two male thralls reached for their guns.

"Gun," I whispered to Jagger.

I shoved away. Backflipped. Came to my feet faster than any normal human ever could. Jagger, my thrall, had already turned and fired. As I rose upright, the Hells Angel thrall crumpled into the dirt, a hand on his abdomen.

The men at the table dove to safety.

"Nobody move," McQuestion shouted.

But it was already too late. Every biker on the premises had a weapon drawn. Most of them were pointed at Jagger and me. I stood slowly, my hands raised.

"He drew on you," Jagger said to McQuestion.

"I drew on the bitch." The gray-bearded man pointed at me. And began to gasp. Blood pulsed out from beneath his hand. Razor and the Sabbath pointed guns at the men at the table. At me.

"Asshole," I said, warning in my tone.

"Jacopo," Marconi said, his voice calm, too soft to carry beyond the table of standing enemies. "Leg shots. Take them."

Two shots rang out.

Jacopo had holstered his weapon before anyone else had time to blink. The Sabbath fell, grabbing his leg, dropping his weapon. Razor had moved. I didn't think it was possible, but Jacopo had missed. Her nanobots and augmentation had defeated nearly superhuman skill.

The wounded Sabbath dropped his weapon, his transitioning not far enough along to force him to keep fighting.

Then, Spy sent me a vision of the woman.

She and her mate, Maul, were perched over Razor's head as she hid behind my flatbed. I sent Spy a vision of jumping her and scratching her bloody. Spy sent back a smug feeling. She and Maul dropped onto Razor.

Cat screams and a woman's guttural shout rang on the air. Razor and a ball of furious cats tumbled into sight.

Blood flew. I felt Spy take a cut along her side. She leaped away.

Razor grabbed Maul, ripped his claws out of her face, and threw the cat against the armored side of my truck. The door dented. Maul fell and lay still.

Heat, fury, and hate thumped once, hard, through my bloodstream. Into my bones.

Razor met my eyes across the space. Faster than human, she ran at me, her bloodied blade held in her left hand.

I shoved off. One foot landed on top of the round table. Shot glasses and good tequila went flying.

Second step hit the ground on the far side. Passing

McQuestion. Racing at her.

My bloodstream pumped hard, telling me, *enemy, enemy, enemy*.

My eyes dilated. I saw everything at once. Everyone still had weapons drawn, moving back and forth, covering everyone else.

This would be a bloodbath. Unless—

I dove-leaped-bounded. Seemingly flying. In midair I shifted position. Tightened my left arm, bracing my shoulder. Blocked her left-handed weapon with my right forearm. Hit her with my left shoulder, momentum, body mass in flight. Direct hit. High in her gut.

She *oofed* out a breath.

I grabbed her wrist with my right hand as we fell. Landed, my momentum driving my shoulder deeper between her ribs.

A strangled sound gagged from her.

I rolled. Yanked back her little finger. Broke it. Took the knife. Shoved it slightly into the flesh of her carotid. She went still. Only her breath heaving. Our faces were centimeters apart, her face and neck covered with cat scratches. Her blood called to me to kill her. I made a fist around the knife hilt and punched her hard, instead. Breaking teeth. The metal bits in my gloves raked her mouth, tearing her flesh.

Tears filled her eyes. "Bitch."

I grinned, showing teeth and fury. I lay my bare left wrist, above my glove, against a cat scratch on her face. I shoved with my nanobots. Claiming her.

She writhed and I shoved the knife tip deeper into the cut in her neck. "One millimeter. Maybe two. And you're dead." She went still, her eyes promising retribution.

Amos sauntered over to me and used plastic ties to secure Razor. The ties were enough to hold a gorilla. I hoped they'd be enough for her.

I passed the knife to Amos and rolled off Razor, keeping my wrist on her face.

"Amos, you and Cupcake get a standard MBB out for the gut-shot male, fast. Put a pneumatic tourniquet and Xstat treatments into the other guy's leg wound. And put Maul and Spy into our vet-bay."

My two thralls leaped onto the flatbed. Without mechanical help, Amos strong-armed one of the triage battlefield med-bays to the ground and Cupcake flipped a switch to turn it on. Together they lifted the gut-shot man into the MBB, closed the top, and set it to stabilize. Amos handed down the vet-bay. Cupcake picked up the limp cat and carried Maul to it.

Amos then knelt at the Sabbath's side and assisted with emergency treatment.

As if I hadn't just had a fight, I said calmly to the club leaders, "You boys want to know why your number-two enforcer and two made-men drew on a peaceful negotiation?"

They looked pissed, so I raised my voice slightly, drawing all the attention to me. "I can give you that information."

"How?" Whip's voice was quiet, demanding.

"The device at my thigh," I answered softly. I nudged out a hip to indicate it.

The leaders, who had scattered during the fight, moved closer to us, watching each other, watching Razor and me with icy, violent, threatening eyes.

I had to take control of this situation. I shouted to the assembled, "There are traitors among you, like Razor and the two with her. Poisoned. Infected by Clarisse Warhammer and forced to obey her. I know how to find them and stop them. I can make them well again. Put down your weapons."

No one moved, but no one fired. Tension wasn't rising, but it wasn't mellowing to campfires and singing "Kumbaya," either.

"I'm betting every leader here has a traitor in their midst," I said, softer. "Probably more than one. Get everyone to stand down."

None of the dozens of weapons were holstered except Jacopo's, but still, no one else had fired. I took that as my cue and said, "I. Can. Prove. It."

I smelled Warhammer on Razor's blood, but that wasn't proof I could offer.

"I'm getting up." Slowly, I rolled to my knees. "I'm pulling the device." I eased the nano detector from my pocket, activated it, and showed it to the men. I bent over Razor, at the unbloodied side of her throat, then pressed it against her skin at her carotid. The green light turned red, and the gauge hit at about 75.

"She's got antibodies." I meant nanobots, but explaining that would take forever. "She's poisoned," I said. When I stood up, I wasn't surprised to find every weapon on me. My voice steady, lower, I continued, "I can prove it. Jacopo. Your arm."

Jacopo hesitated only a moment before rolling up his sleeve and extending his arm. I pressed the start button. Jacopo tested at zero nanobots. "Green. No antibodies. He's not infected."

Marconi met my eyes and walked to me. Extended his wrist.

I tested him and said, "Green."

Whip held out his wrist.

I tested the prez of the Hells Angels. "Green."

I then tested the other leaders. Then the man in the med-bay. He was a hard 70. The one with the leg-shot was only at 25, still transitioning.

"And you?" Whip demanded.

"I'm positive. All my people are because we were similarly poisoned. Antibodies are still in our systems. But the queen who infected me is dead." Surely the bicolor queen who infected me was long gone. It was over ten years ago. "I'm my own person, not a slave to someone else. Because I figured out how to defeat it." I pressed the detector against my neck. I redlined at 100.

Marconi's son Enrico—pretty, oh-so-Italian Enrico—stepped up. In his new Berger-chip-created Italian accent, he said, "I was infected by the Warhammer. This woman"—he indicated me with a graceful gesture—"she cure me. I no longer hear Warhammer's blood calling me to come to her. I am my father's man again."

I waited for him to say he wanted to be with me instead, but he stepped back.

"So we need to make sure Warhammer is stopped? Neutralized?" Marconi asked.

"Killed. Yeah," I said. "Then the problem is solved. Forever."

Without waiting for the leaders to process all that had

happened in the last few minutes, I said, "Amos. As soon as the cats are okay, knock Razor out and put her in the vet-bay. Set the program to cleanse, start Berger chips, and the proper fluids and meds." Each time I spoke, I lowered my voice, letting it say for me that I had this under control, that no one needed to do anything or kill anyone.

"Copy that, Shining."

To the leaders, I said, "You have choices to make."

Whip and Marconi exchanged looks with McQuestion. Bengal and Mama-Killer each nodded.

Keeping one eye on Amos and Cupcake and one on the assembled, I said, "Don't let anyone fire. It's what War-hammer wants. Don't let anyone leave. Any other infected will want to get away if they can't make us fight each other."

Casually, McQuestion shouted, "OMW weapons down! At ease. Nobody leaves. Anybody tries to leave without a direct order from me will be shot dead."

Each of the others called out the same.

The weapons disappeared, but my eyes caught the furtive movements of a number of people. *Bloody hell.* There had to upward of twenty infected.

Whip tilted his head to the side, and all the leaders stepped away into a tight group. Whatever they said was short and sweet. When they came back to me, Whip said, "Test every man and woman here. Start with Hells Angels."

This is where it would get dicey. All my people were positive. Jagger was positive, too. Ever since I heard about the nano tester I had been shuffling through ideas on how to keep him safe, and had decided it would have to be situational.

To Marconi, Whip said, "Secure any who test positive. Shoot any who run."

"Can you make the infected talk?" Marconi asked me.

"No. But she can." I lifted a hand to Mina, who stood about two meters away. No one but me had seen her ap-proach. The psycho was as stealthy as a cat.

Mina smiled, just the tiniest bit. And *bloody hell* it was a scary smile.

"I'll test Mina first," I said, "then Camilla. We can work through the HAs together. Then the OMWs. I'll toss a coin for Black Sabbath and Boozefighters."

"Heads," the Booze prez said, "for first testing."

I pulled an old US quarter and tossed it. Caught the coin and slapped it onto my glove. It showed tails up. "Boozefighters will be tested last."

Whip nodded. "Then we talk. Until we know who our own people are, we'll drink. Maybe play a little Five Card Stud."

I wasn't going to get a better deal. "Jacopo Marconi, Mina Marconi, Camilla Gamble. To me."

*
*

Marconi's other children and McQuestion's daughter tested negative.

Then I told them what reactions to watch for in those waiting to be tested: fear, anger, shifty eyes that calculated a way out, that stared at someone they wanted to kill, or indicated a desire to run. They had an easy job. When I approached the HAs, four people took off. Mina brought them down with small throwing knives, hamstringing or hitting them in their glutes faster than I could follow.

The four were infected—one woman and three men, none of them Marconi's. He had learned how to protect his people. Whip, however, was seriously pissed that he had spies in his organization.

Jacopo and Camilla left the blades in place and secured the infected people's wrists.

The OMW had a higher number of thralls—seven in total, five of them male.

Warhammer liked owning men.

McQuestion sat with his back to the action, but I could read fury in the lines of his body.

While we worked, Jolene took encrypted intel off each infected biker's Morphon, including evidence of Gov., military, and Hand of the Law infiltration in all the biker clubs. I had everything. Names in the Gov. Names and ranks in the military. Cops in every town. Contact info and bios of them all. Our enemies were everywhere. Warhammer's nest was spreading faster than I had believed possible. And Jolene was absorbing it all into her databanks.

As the Marconi scions subdued the OMWs, I turned to Jagger and said, "Your turn." He met my eyes and held my gaze as I pressed the nano-detector against his skin. Without pushing the button. "You're clean, Asshole," I said loud enough so the Marconis could hear me.

"Of course I'm clean. And my name is Jagger. Logan Jagger."

"I like Asshole better."

Jagger laughed and the sound went through me like melted butter and warm maple syrup. My nanos wanted to rip off his armor and take him on the ground. I stepped away from temptation and went back to work.

It took until near sunset before all the infected were sequestered. By then, Razor was in our personal med-bay. Spy was hissing mad, but fine. Maul might limp with pain until he could get back into the vet-bay for a second go-round, but his ribs were stitching together and his broken legs were mending. He could get around. His cracked skull was a different matter, making him dizzy, and that would take several stints in the vet-bay. I would treat him again when Razor was done.

When the last thrall was isolated, one of the noninfected came forward about her man, who was zip-tied and secured to a tree. She told me all about how they had met this woman. Warhammer's image was on his Morphon. The Old Lady hadn't told her prez because her man told her not to and backed it up with a fist to her jaw. When I heard that, I walked to her Old Man, adjusted my gloves so the pointed steel knuckle rivets were in the right places, made a good fist, and punched him directly in his mouth. He was laughing as my fist came at him because I was a little girl in name as well as in reality. But I was stronger than human.

Only as my fist impacted his jaw did I realize I had just usurped the power and job of an enforcer. I busted out his front teeth, tore his lips, and gave him a serious case of whiplash.

Behind him, I spotted a woman slinking from tree to tree. Down the road. Getting away. *Bloody damn*. It was McQuestion's Old Lady. Six-Gun Annie Gamble. This would get ugly.

I walked over to Jagger. Hiding my gesture, I pointed. "McQuestion's Old Lady hasn't been tested. She's trying to escape."

Jagger cursed.

"I'm going after her. You deal with your boss." I raised my voice, shouting as I tore down the drive, "Cupcake! To me!"

She was instantly at my left side, keeping pace. My nanobots reached out to her, connecting. I felt her armor harden, her attention shift for an instant. I saw what she saw.

Knowing what she planned, I held out my hand for the weapon she placed into it. Synchronicity at its finest. I slowed.

Cupcake passed me. Using her armor's reverse recoil feature, she leaped two meters up.

I fired at a man partially hidden behind a nearby tree in the same moment that Cupcake grabbed a tree limb overhead. Swung forward and landed on Annie's back. They rammed into a pile of dry dead limbs. Cupcake flipped the woman over and slapped her once. Into unconsciousness.

When my target went down, I walked over, kicked away his sniper's rifle, and shot him again, outer left arm, the round tearing into his delt. I toed him over and saw where my first shot had taken him through the right shoulder. Blood spurted. My round had hit him low enough to have nicked his lung and the big artery that fed his arm. He'd bleed out in two minutes. I tried to decide if I cared. He stank of Warhammer. I was pretty sure he wasn't alone. I decided I had other priorities.

He whimpered, gasped, and died.

I walked over and stared down at Annie, who had just complicated my life. She was coming around faster than she would have, had she been a normal human.

Jagger was coming up behind me. He wasn't alone. I set my expression into battlefield neutral and met McQuestion's eyes. At his side was his daughter. Tears were running down her face.

"She isn't dead, Camilla," I said, my tone neutral. "Just knocked silly." *Concussion, possible brain damage, and a traitor to you and your dad and your club*, I thought. Annie shook her head, trying to wake up.

"Roy, you wanted to know how Warhammer found out about today?" I said. "Here's your answer."

Camilla stepped into her father's arms, still sobbing.

"Please, Daddy. Please," she whispered.

Grief etched Roy's face as he cradled his daughter's head against his kutte. I didn't understand. Then he pulled a weapon. "I said if anyone ran, they'd be shot," he said. "You ran."

"Roy, no!" Annie said, struggling to form the words. "I can explain—"

He fired. Three shots. Into his wife's chest. Her breath exhaled. She lay still.

Roy walked away, pulling his daughter as if in a dance step. He shot the sniper as they walked past, though the man was already dead. He holstered his weapon, back straight, his body taut.

I stood there, lips parted, breathing too fast, trying to reason out what had just happened.

"He didn't know his Old Lady had been infected when he said he'd shoot anyone who ran," Cupcake said as she lifted Annie in her arms, carrying her like a baby. "And when she ran, he didn't have a choice."

"Everyone has a choice," I said as we walked toward the rig.

I knew one thing. I was firmly back in the biker world. And no matter how this ended up, people were going to die. And I was screwed.

*

*

Locking the cats out of the back of the cab, I cleaned up in the truck, trying to wand off the stink of skewed honor, misplaced promises, and the blood and stench of War-hammer's thralls. I used some of our precious water to wash off any of her nanobots that might have been lurking on Annie's skin.

I had killed the sniper in cold blood, and I wasn't upset by that in the least. But Six-Gun Annie's death and Camil-la's tears, and even the memory of the brown-eyed woman I had killed at the beginning of all this, had unleashed something in me. Something bitter and miserable. It had been compounded by the bleak purpose in Roy's eyes as he carried out his promise.

I pulled on clean underwear, but had no clean jeans, no clean shirt. I tried the wand on the cloth, but all it did was turn the blood black. When I was decent, I opened the tiny door to see Spy sitting like some Egyptian goddess on the back of the passenger seat, her odd eyes—one bright green, the other bright blue—on mine. I figured she wanted to chat, and though I didn't want anyone's mind in mine, I plopped down in the narrow space between the seats and stared at her.

"I know you think me being upset about Roy killing Annie is stupid, but there's something about it that stuck me right here." I tapped my chest. "Did you know that my father sent me into the bowels of a Mama-Bot war machine, carrying a mini-nuke in my backpack?" Tears gathered in my eyes. "It was pink. The backpack. Not the nuke." I laughed, a single bark that sounded just a little crazy. "My own father. What kind of person does that? What kind of person sends his little girl into the heart of the enemy?" I shook my head. "I'll tell you what kind of person. The same kind who kills his own wife in front of his daughter just to save face, just to keep a promise and a threat."

Spy continued to watch me, her eyes steady, unblinking. She sat tall, her front feet together and her tail wrapped around them. Regal. Like the queen she would become when Tuffs died or stepped down.

"That's part of the reason I left the OMW after Pops died. I knew I'd infect and kill the people I loved. I was so tired of war. So tired of that macho bullshit way of life. So I ran away. To a junkyard. Running from one macho business to another. I guess I didn't run far from the lifestyle, did I? Basically, I'm a big tangled ball of mixed-up emotions and screwed-up thinking patterns. In my own way, I'm worse than Roy." I laughed again, that horrid broken noise, and wiped snot and tears off my face. Crying was foreign. Unexpected. "I killed Pops trying to save him. I swore I'd never transition anyone ever again, but I did when I saved Mateo. And Grant Zuckerman, because I was lonely. Did you know his bones are still underneath some John Deere tractors?" My breath hitched on a sob.

Spy didn't respond. Her tail tip twitched once.

"I transitioned Mateo. Cupcake and Amos and Jagger. Enrico. And Tuffs, though to give myself at least a little credit, I had no idea that I could transition a cat. And Amos asked to be changed. And Jagger was just in the wrong place at the wrong time. Fine. I have some excuses. But"—I looked out the windshield, seeing only a square of sky—"I broke my own promises. Then there was Wanda. Alex. And now Razor, just because I wanted to show her who was boss."

So far, I hadn't touched anyone here except Razor. Part of me hoped she wouldn't survive her second transition. Another part was ashamed that I had that thought.

Spy tilted her head and one ear twitched. Her odd eyes studied me.

I wiped another tear off my cheek. "I'm talking to a cat that would eat my dead body if I died. Yeah. Right. Thanks for listening. You got something to say?"

Spy dropped to one of my thighs, which were curled in the yoga position, and stood, her front paws on my chest. She lowered her head and waited.

I put my forehead to her furry, fuzzy one, and the world around me swirled, went dizzy, shifted sideways. Nausea rose, but my world stabilized before I gagged and vomited, so that was good.

In Spy's strange greenish cat vision, which had no reds and very little yellow, I saw six clowders of cats, each clowder sitting in a tight group in a space that was mostly fog or clouds. Fog was rare enough that I knew the cat groupings were figurative or perhaps allegorical in some way that was important to Spy, but was not reality or an actual memory as I understood those things. The clowders were arranged in a circle, each led by a female, each group facing the center.

In that center was Tuffs.

There was something odd about the circle of cats, with Tuffs as the heart of their universe. In another time, with other creatures, the six points might actually have suggested a star, the kind used in magic or religion or geometry. Since it was cats, and they had indicated no affinity to magic, no religious leanings, and I hadn't caught them doing algebra or geometry, I figured it was coincidence.

Spy sent me a picture of one group of cats getting up from the circle and walking through the fog to Marconi. It was an odd overlay of allegorical vision and reality that made my stomach roil again. Another group of cats stood and walked to Whip. Yet another group walked to McQuestion, whose hands displayed a delicate tremor, a vibration of pain. His body stank of grief. I hadn't realized that grief had a scent. The next two groups of cats joined Bengal and Mama-Killer. Spy walked to me. In her thoughts I was identified by the smell of salmon and milk and the scuffed leather of my work boots.

I pulled my head back, breaking the close mental communication, and met Spy's eyes. "Tuffs wants a team in each club? She thinks she can keep an eye on the bikers, can keep tabs on my . . . on *our* friends and enemies. She knows they'll be hundreds of kilometers apart, right?"

Spy stared at me in that way that meant I had stated the obvious.

"I guess Tuffs has already put her plan into action," I groused at Spy. "That's why all the cats are here in the first place."

It was an excellent plan, and if a human had come up with it, I'd think it was bloody brilliant. The fact that a cat had come up with it was bloody scary. The fact that Tuffs believed she could communicate with her thralls and nest mates through such a distance was bloody terrifying.

"I can't stop the cats from going with the clubs. But if they go, they might be used in dog-baiting events. If they go and are injured or get sick, no one will be there to set up a vet-bay for them. They could die far from home. Alone."

Spy agreed. *"Hhhhah mmm."* The sound stretched out, longer than usual, followed by *"Orrrowmerow,"* the sound that meant *this is a bad problem.*

I figured that meant they all understood the dangers of leaving home. "I won't be able to make the clubs agree to take cats. If Tuffs and you want to do this, you'll have to figure it out on your own."

Spy bowed her head again and shoved it against mine.

I saw a vision of the bikers' Old Ladies, cats on their laps, stroking the invaders, whose tails were twitching slowly. The cats had charmed the women—black and white, young and old—and because cats could suss out who had the most power in a group of humans, they had bonded with the leaders' Old Ladies or children. I chuckled again, and this time I almost sounded like me. "The cats have already insinuated their way into the different clubs. Figures. Question. Is Tuffs planning on taking over the world?"

Spy sent me an image of dozens of cats sitting in luxury, being fed fresh raw shrimp by besotted humans. And then a vision of Spy telling Tuffs, and then me, what was happening. "So, you're in charge of the actual spy groups, and you intended to report back to me?" If I was understanding this right, through the cats I might have access to what was going on in all the biker organizations.

"*Hhhhah mmm,*" Spy agreed, and broke contact.

I washed my face, smeared on fresh sunscreen and the orange lipstick, and set my orange sunglasses in place. Opening the cab door, I leaped to the ground. Looking up at Spy on the passenger seat I said, "It's up to Tuffs, the individual cats, and the Old Ladies."

Spy and her clowder cats, who had been sitting on the running boards, leaped to the ground and wove around my feet. In the distance, I heard gunshots. Gently, I shut the cab door and jogged behind cover, to a spot where I could see the fortress. More gunshots sounded.

If the clubs had gone to war with each other, it would be stupid to charge in. Same if they were just shooting beer bottles. If they were killing their infected members, there wasn't much I could do about it. "Cupcake," I asked into my comms system, "what's going on?"

"One of the Old Ladies pulled a knife on another one, and they ended up brawling in the dirt. Their men pulled guns and fired them into the air. I nearly had a heart attack, but no one's dead."

"Why were they fighting?"

"They both wanted the same cat."

"Bloody *damn.*" I looked around for Spy, but she was suddenly nowhere in sight. I muttered, "Cats do not have magic. They cannot make humans fall in love with them." But I remembered the circle of circles, six groups of cats, and the queen in the center. That could be construed as a metaphysical seven and the use of magical power. It could also be an indication that the cats wanted me to make a bigger nest, just as Tuffs had.

I was pretty sure I was slipping off the road into some

form of delusional insanity.

"Cupcake, get the vids ready. Now that the thralls are weeded out and the club leaders have seen the trade stuff"—*and the blasted cats are causing trouble*, I added to myself—"we need to tell them what we want and let them see the cats in action."

*

*

There have been times in my life when my worldview broke, fracturing into millions of sharp, cutting, jagged edges that left me bleeding. The first time was when the first Mama-Bot crawled out of Possession Sound, Washington, and began destroying everything in its path. The second time was when Little Mama, my mother, took a hit while riding sidecar next to Pops. One minute she was firing at enemy troops; the next she had rocked back in the sidecar, dead. I had never told anyone, but I'd managed to steal the video of her death from Pops and had watched it over and over, bits of me dying along with her each time I watched. The third time was when the bicolor ants swarmed me and I should have died. The worst time of all, when my worldview broke and fell apart, was when I tried to heal and save Pops by transitioning him, and he died instead. There were more, but, to me, a shifting worldview always meant trauma, pain, and death.

When I watched the leaders' faces as Cupcake narrated Spy's and Maul's reconnoiter of Warhammer's bunker, I saw another way for worldviews to change.

Pulling a rabbit out of your hat doesn't always mean doing magic, finding a rabbit, or even having a hat. It means making others believe you had done what you claimed they were seeing. And the cats were seemingly taking orders, working as a team, and using rational thought processes to solve problems, which went against a human worldview.

Worse for them was watching rats walk in lockstep, attacking the cats.

The Boozefighter Henry Thibodaux, AKA Bengal, said, "Them rats. They workin' together." Despite the name, I hadn't known he was Cajun until he let down his guard and his childhood accent came flooding back. His dark eyes were on the cats, watching them run away from the rats, which were attacking in a near-military line. "Big as nutria, they is." He shifted his eyes to me, where I stood in the corner of the poker room in the fortified, repaired house. "That 'cause they infected too?"

I jutted my chin. "Yes."

"That all got to die. I'm in if we kill all them rats."

The Black Sabbath leader, J'Ron Walker, AKA Mama-Killer, said, "I seen things big as that in the old subway tunnels. But rats walking like troops is fucking bad." He looked at Bengal and then to me. "I want to hear the plan, but unless it's fucking nuts, I'm in."

Whip, of the Hells Angels, made a cutting motion with one hand and the vid froze on a closeup of Spy's odd eyes in Maul's camera. He swiveled in his chair to me. "The cats are working together too. Why? Cats never work as a team."

I let a bargaining look enter my eyes; it was a combination of knowing more than I was telling, and being willing to share some.

"The rats were turned by Warhammer."

"And the cats?" Whip asked.

"Theirs is a unique mutation," I lied, then added a bit of truth. "They eat toxic rats and bats. And they also ate a few of Warhammer's members." I shrugged at the expression on Whip's face. "But the cats don't answer to her. They don't answer to anyone, hence the unique mutation. They do, however, work with a team if they feel like it. Cats view their providers as servants and their enemies as protein. It's efficient." They also considered their servants, should they pass away, as protein, but I was too canny a bargainer to say that.

"The cats' mutations left them more like a pride of lions than housecats. It also gave them the ability to understand English, and I've been talking to them. A lot. The cats are still independent, like all cats, but if the bargain is good enough, they'll work with, and as, a team. What you're seeing is the cats' willingness to understand a problem and work together because the bargain was good enough." I grinned just a little. "Bargains with cats always have a protein component. But this time, they want the rats destroyed too, so it's a win-win for them."

"The cats talked to you? Told you that?" Whip asked,

amusement in his tone but speculation in his eyes.

"Not with words, no. Remember the rat Spy dropped on the table when I first got here? That was her . . . call it her *proof of status*. Best hunter in the pride. Proof she can take down huge rats. In biker terms she's the president's heir and runs her own chapter house."

Whip studied me for a little too long before he swiveled his chair to Cupcake and pointed at the screen for us to continue. When the vids had been studied long enough for the leaders to all understand the need to take Warhammer down, see what prizes were on the table, and get a feel for the layout of the bunker, Marconi ordered the food be served and we got down to bargaining. I couldn't take off my gloves and eat, for fear of infecting someone with my nanobots, so I made an excuse, and Cupcake brought me warm broth to sip, which I could do with my gloves on.

No one cared that I didn't eat. The leaders ignored me, which was fine by me. I didn't have to offer much, not after they watched the vids. Their own people turning against them and the lockstep of the rats was enough to create a temporary alliance. The potential spoils in the bunker cemented it. All I had to do was throw in some Dragon Scale armor and some of the blasters from the containers I got from Marty's foundry when I discovered his part in Harlan's death.

The only sticking point for agreement to attack the bunker was the lack of heavy artillery.

"I am not attacking a war bunker with handguns and blasters, and without military backup," Whip said. "And if we do bring in the military, they'll just take their bunker back when we're done. We'll have nothing. This meeting is a waste of time."

That one point—admittedly a pretty major one—also had Mama-Killer standing and ready to ride off into the sunset.

Jagger looked at me, amusement on his mouth. *Bloody damn*, there was so much I wanted to do with that mouth. And the rest of him. My nanobots stirred.

Unless Jagger had told McQuestion, no one knew about the Simba or the warbot. I had to assume that all of Jagger's memories had returned, and that my mind-wipe, when he was transitioned, had fallen apart. Yeah, he had probably told his boss. Which was why McQuestion was still sitting. And Marconi probably knew about the Simba from witnesses at the camp where we salvaged it, which meant that Whip knew.

"Stop," I said. "Wait." I slipped my comms back into my ears and tapped a small depression. "Now."

"Now *what*?" Marconi asked, too knowingly, his expression sly.

Slowly, drawing their attention to every movement I made, I stood and walked to the huge window looking over the hills behind the armored house. "Now *this*."

The men gathered in front of me, elbowing me to the side. Which was fine with me, because I got to watch their faces when Mateo drove the Simba down the hills and toward the back entrance, narrowly missing crushing Marconi's bikes. With the camo feature turned off, it was like watching an entire city block crush across the landscape on tank tracks. Then it stopped. The Simba sat there, in all its mid-war glory, clearly not a piece of scrap, but a war machine with functional weapons.

Mateo didn't have to get out, so the fact that the driver was a warbot was still a secret. A partial secret. Maybe.

In the poker room, no one moved until Bengal swiveled on his feet and demanded, "What the fuck else you got hid?"

"Not much as you hope. Maybe more than I've said."

The Booze and the Sabbath glared at each other, looked back out the window, and both shrugged. "I'm in," they both said.

The Simba's chameleon skin wavered, and it disappeared, visible only by the movement of crushed trees as it crawled up the far hill on its massive tracks.

"And you want nothing out of this bunker except a prisoner, right?" McQuestion asked.

"Like I said. You let me rescue her as part of this Op, you help me kill Warhammer, and you can have all the goodies."

All in all, the leaders reached a consensus much faster than I had expected. I had come prepared for us to stay overnight if necessary, but after seeing the Simba—and the execution of McQuestion's wife—the club leaders were all in. Part of their easy acquiescence might have been the grief, poorly hidden in McQuestion's eyes. Part of it was the rats. Part was seeing how many of their own people had been infected. And part was all the wartime weapons, armaments, supplies, and goodies in the bunker. But the biggest part was the men's abilities to see a problem and decide when to be practical and pragmatic and work together for a common goal.

Plus, they knew they could kill each other afterward if needed.

*

*

It was dead-dark-thirty when the biker leaders finally hammered out the specifics of their agreement to work together, without honoring their individual supposedly-ultra-secret contracts with the military. The clubs' parley ended with the agreement to keep their infected members in the prison—which Marconi informed us he had discovered in the basement of his fortress—until they could be transitioned back with my med-bay and my "medication protocol." They still needed to choose a commander to run the attack—which I figured they'd fight over, then end up choosing Jagger. Sure enough, the conversation got heated, so I left them to check on the med-bay occupants, my cats, and the prisoners. While I was occupied, they also picked a time and a location to meet—about two klicks south of the bunker in a time schedule I could meet if I hustled. Maybe most important—in an action that showed solidarity with Roy Gamble, who had killed his own wife—they volunteered to shoot their own people at the slightest hint of betrayal.

When I got back, they were done, a bit more bloody and banged up than when I left, but all in agreement, which was way more than I expected. I followed them back downstairs where they each, individually, announced the plan of action to their members, the small groups that I had separated and merged into looser packs, back in place again as they talked with their club members. I had all I wanted and needed. A chance to rescue Evelyn and the promise to kill Warhammer. Nothing else mattered.

And then the leaders shook hands, bumped fists, and packed up. I managed to cover my shock when I was included in the fist bumping, gloves to gloves, but I managed not to make an *eeep* sound like a little girl when it happened.

The clubs dispersed, bikes roaring into the night, taking their part of the supplies and weapons I had offered. And the cats.

Spy and her clowder stayed with me, which was a relief. Spy was adventurous. She was a warrior cat. I had been afraid she might desert me.

Our crew, with Tuffs and Spy's clowder, went back to the junkyard. I held Spy on my lap as Cupcake drove and hummed along with the radio, turned low. She was still off-key but it wasn't as noticeable since she wasn't competing with the radio volume. For most of the trip, my fingers massaged Spy. Then she scratched me. Blasted cat. I sucked my fingers. "You know perfectly well how to tell me to stop. Next time you scratch I'll roll down the window and throw you into the bushes."

She flicked her tail at me, unconcerned, and rolled over, exposing her belly for more scratches, which I ignored. I wasn't risking my flesh again.

"Tuffs was an abandoned cat," I said to Spy. "Maybe she got tossed out of a moving car. You should ask her how it felt."

On the dash, Tuffs opened one eye, held my gaze for five agonizing seconds, and closed it.

I crossed my arms and tried to decide if I was pouting. I probably was, so I concentrated on the good things that had happened: I had intel taken from the traitors' Morphons, an indication of how widespread Warhammer's contagion was, along with names, ranks, addresses, and pics of dozens of her thralls. I had gotten away without touching anyone with my skin except Razor. Without expanding my nest. And without sticking my tongue down Jagger's throat. I had spies in every leader's family and the principal chapter house in every club. If the cats bothered to tell me what was going on, that was an ace up my sleeve. I decided I had come out ahead and fell asleep as the old truck rolled down the back roads, the Simba behind us in stealth mode.

I lurched awake when the truck bounced into the office's driveway and up to the sealed gate, Cupcake working the gears, her voice silent.

Mateo, in the Simba, was in front of us, trundling back into hiding.

Jolene said, "Welcome back, y'all. It's so good to see you all alive. And you brought company too. Now ain't that sweet."

I didn't know that Jagger had followed us until his bike thrummed up the drive and circled around us. He'd been driving lights-off, night-camo mode. I hadn't checked the sensors. Hadn't sensed him. And no one had told me he was following, though they had to have known. All of them.

I swung down from the cab to the ground and met his eyes in the darkness. Heat branded its way through me, thrust into my muscles, seared along my nerves. I turned away for the office. He trailed me, his armored boots nearly silent on the dirt.

I was so tired that I didn't speak when he followed me through the airlocks and secured the doors, locking the cats and my people out of the office. He held my eyes, not speaking, his heated and dark and promising everything. And nothing. I waited in silence as he stepped to the donning station and his armor was removed. He was naked when it fell away, and he stood there, letting me look my fill. Then he walked to me, took my hand, and led me to my bed.

He had promised me it would be, "Mind-blowing. Screaming. Hot. Sweaty. Sex."

He was right.
Bloody hell.
Bloody sodding damn it all to hell.
*
*

The next morning, Jagger eased out of bed before the sun rose. I pretended to be asleep as he crept out through the airlock doors. I wasn't sure what I was feeling or what my nanobots wanted him to feel, and it seemed wiser, as well as safer, to just let him go.

Chicken. We both were chicken.

In a biker club, unless one was legally married or an Old Lady, sex was a casual thing—no love, no romance, no future beyond the tumble in the sheets. But this was something else, something new, at least for me. This felt like . . . more. More of what, I had no idea. And Jagger had gone, as he always would, back to McQuestion, without words or discussions or feelings. I wasn't surprised. I wasn't especially hurt.

But maybe I was numb, just a bit. And very, *very* angry.

As the airlock closed, Spy and Maul, Tuffs and Notch leaped to the bed and snuggled into the warm place where Jagger had rested. Not slept, not last night. But with the cats snuggling around me, nearly as warm as Jagger, I fell into dreamless sleep. And for once, Cupcake didn't wake me for coffee and breakfast.

*
*

Once she no longer had to provide cover for me, I hadn't paid much attention to Wanda and Alex at the negotiations. But after Jagger left and we started preparing for the battle to come, I learned what they had been doing. Alex had been spying on the biker clubs by carrying an oversized, lazy-looking cat around in their arms and listening to the Old Ladies chat among themselves. Alex was an excellent snoop, with a keen eye for details and a great ear for gossip. They also looked innocent, which was not a trait anyone in a biker club was accustomed to.

Wanda, on the other hand, had strolled from group of Old Ladies to group of Old Ladies, facilitating trade; setting up an impromptu swap meet among the women in the clubs; and talking about cats and her fab-o armor. With the female made-men, she chatted about guns, armor, military tech, and knives. Having worked at Morrison's, Wanda knew a lot about weapons and tech. She might not shoot a lot, but she knew the lingo, and the female made-men had needs Wanda was willing to encourage and attempt to fulfill. She made a number of sales and useful trades during the negotiations, a lot of it from my mattress inventory. She also created a new social concept: the Old Ladies and Female Made-Men Party, with booze, stuff to exchange or bargain over, and lively conversation about how horrible men were. I'd had no idea what she was capable of until I heard the details.

She had gathered all the women together and encouraged them to talk. She had listened to the women complain, argue, gripe, and had also watched them fight. Literally. Fists and knives and sword-edged words. Safe and protected in her armor, she had pulled apart the participants of three fights before she realized that wasn't enough. The Old Ladies were about to go to war when Wanda shook two fighting women like cats and ordered them to behave or she'd show them how many teeth a woman in a suit of armor could knock out.

Wanda then began to divide and conquer. She gathered the remaining Old Ladies into a separate spot, got them roaring drunk, and suggested to them that the clubs could and should have quarterly swap meet / meet-and-greet combos, like a summit between heads of state—discussions to avoid future confrontations. She had told them they had more power than they thought, because men would agree to anything after a good tumble, and they could keep their men and their children and their clubs safe if they worked together instead of going to war. They had *power*. It wasn't a foreign concept, but maybe no one had put it to them quite the way Wanda did.

Once she had the Old Ladies happy, she had turned her attention to the female made-men, a much more violent, rugged group. She suggested that the clubs could work together and divide up the nation instead of fighting each other, and then fight the PRC and the Gov. if necessary. She also suggested that the clubs, working together, would have enough power to negotiate with the military from a position of strength instead of taking contracts that put them in danger in return for smaller gains. Female made-men usually liked to fight and were always looking for ways to move up in the hierarchy of the clubs, which meant fighting each other even more than the men. Working together, fighting only the men, they could gain status.

What Wanda suggested was part anarchy, part conquest, part treason. While she hadn't really meant to bond the women together with a long-term goal, she had. She had also managed to pit the clubs against the runaway military authorities and the Gov. Working for Marty had prepared her to take a place in my nest I had never expected.

After she was done fomenting peace and betrayal and treachery all at once, she had provided Cupcake a list of new trade items and lots of intel. Like Cupcake, Wanda was exploring her abilities and talents, natural and nanobot-given, looking for a way to serve me.

My alternative to all the alliances was to transition every human on the planet and rule them like a queen.

Which just gave me the squicks.

*

*

The second day after Jagger—no. The second day after *Asshole* left my bed and my office, Cupcake, Amos, Wanda, Alex, and I had breakfast together, discussing our final preparations for battle. Mateo and Jolene were present via screens and speakers through the ship's EntNu.

Cupcake snapped open her Morphon, and standing like a drill sergeant, said, "CO Mateo. Simba update."

"Simba's city-killer has been removed and placed in the *SunStar* for safekeeping," Mateo replied. "The Simba has been upgraded with all the weapons and defenses I think we'll need, and is currently strapped down with charging stations, armor-donning stations, ammo, long-distance weapons, and up-close-and-personal weapons. We have armaments that can take out precision targets at five kilometers using aerial targeting systems and auto-guided missiles We also have eight bunker busters. They're capable of breaking through an underground bunker to a depth of twenty meters, and, with a one-two punch of delivery systems, can reach to two hundred meters."

I frowned at his image on the screen over the command chair. "Where did we get bunker-buster missiles?"

"It's in the mattress inventory," Cupcake said, amused and proud of herself.

I didn't remember seeing weapons of that size, but then I had only made it halfway through the mattress inventory. I flipped up my Morphon and scrolled through until I saw the last page. Mateo had added eight bunker-buster missiles to my arsenal. How had he . . . ?

Bloody hell.

"Mateo," I said. "These bunker-buster missiles. Where did they come from? And how did you get them?"

"The weapons fall under my purview as CO of *SunStar,* for both fulfilling my mission and assigned objectives, and for any operations required to protect and rescue my crew."

I stared at the image of his misshapen head and decided there was more than a hint of hostility in his body language. If his voice could carry emotional overtones, I had a feeling he'd sound mocking, arrogant, and condescending.

And it pissed me off.

"I saw no weapons in the *SunStar* any time I've been inside," I said.

Jolene said, "Well if you ain't telling, CO Sugah, I will. That man done crawled down into the crevasse and rescued them from the wreckage of the back half of me. Nearly killed himself."

I rubbed my scalp. *I wanted him independent*, I reminded myself. *I wanted this.* But he climbed into a mine crack a thousand-plus feet deep and back out. Multiple times. Carrying weapons. What if he had fallen? How could I have gotten him out? I moved my fist from my head to my chest, rubbing small circles to ease the pressure. It was a motion I had seen Little Mama make as I was growing up.

Then it hit me. I was feeling like a mother. With a kid I had to protect. A kid who was in a space-worthy warbot suit and who had survived battle, a spaceship crash, and being eaten alive by nanobots inside his suit. I totally deserved my emotions. I had a right to them. But they were uncomfortable the way new shoes were uncomfortable—they rubbed the wrong way, didn't quite fit.

Oblivious to my discomfort, Mateo continued. "With Jolene's help I can emplace the bunker busters within two kilometers, target the bunker precisely enough to destroy it, fire them at a prearranged time, and leave the WIMP weapon or power source intact. We'd have to be hell and gone before they fire because the military will see them via satellite cameras. But we have them if we need them."

I wanted to swat Mateo for endangering himself, but I had to agree the risk was worth it. "Will the military be able to trace the missiles to the *SunStar*?"

"Negative. Jolene and I tinkered with all identifiers. Also, if needed, the Simba is equipped with close-range lasers and an MJR blaster which is capable of taking down aircraft, a platoon of warbot-suited warriors, even disabling another Simba should Warhammer have all that in the bunker somewhere our recon cats didn't go. But using the blaster would undoubtedly alert the Gov. and involve the military she has in her pocket, and should be considered a last-ditch response."

"Yeah," I muttered. If the military caught us, especially military she had transitioned, we'd be charged with treason, if not shot outright. We were already walking a fine line. But I didn't say that part out loud.

Jolene took over. "The Simba is provided with one rail gun and jamming devices capable of bringing down remote aircraft. Those can be used at any time without fear of military interest. The spy-sats shouldn't pick them up."

"Through Simba and Jolene in the *SunStar*," Mateo said, "we'll have access to, and the ability to, jam any incoming or outgoing EntNu comms, and any standard radio, laser, satellite, or old-fashioned cell-type communications. We have Maarsies and two portable IGPs for killing War-hammer's nanobots. Simba and I are both equipped with the military's best Chameleon skin for traveling unseen, and a dark mode that decreases the Simba's noise to nearly nothing."

"We can travel by day now?" I asked.

"Negative," Mateo said, "unless we're absolutely certain we're a klick or more from any human or electronic observation. Or being chased. Even the interactive camo doesn't stop tracks on dirt roads and the movement of trees. The Simba is invisible by day only when it's not moving. Otherwise we'll be tracked and caught."

Cupcake was watching me, her expression apprehensive, her blue eyes on my Morphon and its mattress inventory. I often forgot that Cupcake still needed to please me. "Good job, you guys. And good job on the weapons inventory, Cupcake. It would have made a quartermaster weep with joy."

Cupcake blushed a pretty pink.

Mateo and Jolene continued the Op planning, detailing logistics and timing, which were going to suck even more on this trip than the last one. "Just like the trip back last time, everyone will be riding in or on the Simba," Mateo said. "ATVs strapped on unless or until we need them. We attracted attention last time, and odds are they'll be watching closer than normal for incursions near the Gov. center."

"Y'all will avoid Interstates 64 and 77 from Naoma, West Virginia," Jolene said, naming the town closest to the junkyard, "heading south to Wytheville, Virginia. Like Mateo said, your only travel should be by night, and even then I suggest y'all need to avoid most secondary and some tertiary roads. Your trip time needs to include sitting in a copse of trees or pile of rubble and hidin' out when the sun is up."

"Maneuvering the Simba parallel to the back roads and overland," Mateo said, "allows us to travel in such a way that we leave no trail. Unfortunately, it also means triple power output, and even with the MPP engines, it will be a strain—triple the prewar klicks, and a longer travel time. Think of our last trip as the warm and cozy version. We'll be moving from tank tracks to mobile support struts and back depending on the terrain and the weather, which is expected to be sunny and hotter than hell by day, cloudless and cold as shit by night. Jolene?"

"After studying the sat-maps I borrowed from the military feed, I'm estimatin' twenty-four hours' actual travel time for y'all to cover the distance, again with all of it after dark. That means y'all have to leave soon to reach the rendezvous point on time."

Three nights to get there. I blinked at the time involved and leaned forward to study the current sat-map on the wall screen and the different proposed routes. We had avoided detection the first time by luck. I didn't believe luck hit twice. So . . . yeah. We had to be smarter when we crossed over the state lines into Virginia.

I turned to Wanda. "What about you and Alex?"

"Alex and I will be staying behind with Jolene to protect and care for the junkyard and the cats," Wanda said. "And . . ." She stopped and turned her head away. "We're both feeling a little sickly. Just like we did when we transitioned." Wanda turned her penetrating gaze back to me. "Are we transitioning again?"

I looked at the kid, who was petting a juvenile cat and listening to everything with that feigned inattention that kids used when they were faking tuning out adult conversation. I'd used that same device when I was their age.

Twelve.

No kid should have to go into battle.

The cat in Alex's lap looked at me. It was the yellow-eyed Little Kitten, the cat who thought she could take over from Tuffs and Spy. I looked around and also saw Little Kitten's clowder, the juveniles inspecting my living place and my seat of power. I wasn't sure why Tuffs had allowed Little Kitten and her pals into the office, and I also wasn't dumb enough to fall for the cat just adopting the kid out of love, but Jolene had eyes everywhere in the junkyard, so Alex and Wanda would be safe. I hoped.

"Shining?" Cupcake asked.

"Yes. There were PRC nanobots in the Simba. We all went through an additional transition. I had hoped you two wouldn't have to, but—" I stopped and rubbed my chest with a fist again, fighting the pressure building there. "I'm sorry."

Alex grinned at me before sliding sly eyes at their mother. "Shit happens."

"Alex," Wanda said, admonishment in her tone.

Alex giggled and hugged LK. The kitten didn't scratch them, so points to the juvie cat.

I said, "The cats who want to come with us. Where do they ride?"

"Inside the Simba with me," Mateo replied. "They'll need protein and a cat box."

"Speaking of which. No cats in the office while I'm gone," I said. "Wanda will provide protein, kibble, and water as per the usual schedule." I set my eyes on Little Kitten. "Any cat who tries to enter by stealth or diversion will be neutered when we get back and put on half rations for two weeks after. We clear, Little Kitten?"

She showed me her hind quarters, which drew Tuffs's attention. The queen cat looked from the juvenile to me and narrowed her eyes. Slowly the Guardian Cat stood and walked across the table to the young cat in Alex's lap. Deliberately she stepped down onto Little Kitten and stood there, looking away, as if unaware she had pinned the smaller cat. Little Kitten's ears went back, and she showed me her fangs, hissing. Tuffs turned her eyes to the smaller juvenile cat and leaned into her. Touching her.

Little Kitten's snarl disappeared. Her body went rigid. Her hair stood on end.

Tuffs raised her head and, moving faster than I could follow, bit Little Kitten's ear hard enough to pierce the skin. Tuffs held the cat in place with her fangs. Two beads of blood appeared.

Slowly, Little Kitten's shoulders hunched and her body flattened on Alex's lap. A good three seconds later, LK went limp.

"Wow," Alex said, their own eyes wide.

Tuffs released LK's ear.

Little Kitten sprang off Alex's lap, leaped across the room, and leaned her whole body against the airlock door. Wanda opened the door, and all of the kitten's clowder departed, tails low, feet almost flying.

"Well, now, that was mighty interestin'," Jolene said.

I had a weird moment of curiosity. Could I do that—whatever *that* had been—to an enemy? Or . . . could I scare off an unwanted thrall? "Yeah. It was." I scowled. "Jolene, if I told you to bomb a small city, would you do it?"

"Hey-yell no."

I laughed. "Good. Mateo. When do we leave?"

"Today. Dark."

I said "Done" and shooed my nest out of the office. Alone, I took a deep breath and said, "Gomez? You there?"

"Indeed."

"Disconnect from Jolene."

"Now wait a minute. That's my fella you're—" Jolene's tirade stopped.

"Done, Shining."

I hadn't talked to the office AI in weeks. There was something creepy about airlock doors suitable for interstellar, intragalactic space travel, a comms chair big enough for several humans, and talking to an alien AI. Creepy enough that I tended to avoid it.

"Thank you." I wasn't sure how polite I needed to be to Gomez, so opting on the side of very polite manners was smart. "Secure the airlock doors, please." I heard the suction sound as the doors sealed tight enough for space travel.

"Secured."

"I'm going downstairs."

"Do you wish to use the feline pathway or your previous method?"

I stopped, my hand a hair's breadth from the handle that opened to a sharply angled chute to the lower levels. "The cats have a way in?" Little crawly phantom fear-spiders scampered across my flesh.

"Indeed." The command chair rotated silently into the command center, leaving that part of the floor empty. "If you press the small black button in the center of the floor, a panel will open, and a stairway will be visible. Lighting will appear as you descend. It is my impression that the wavelength is too dim for human eyes, though the felines had no difficulties. Now that I know humans have such poor vision, I have devised methods to increase the illumination if you wish."

"Yes. Ahhh. Thank you." I spotted the black mark on the floor where the command chair usually sat, an oval with notches. It wasn't a button as I would describe it, or a knob. It wasn't raised, and it felt prickly to my fingers, but when I pressed the rough black oval, the section of the floor around it slid open to reveal a black nothingness that led to more black nothingness.

"When you are below the level of this deck, the access will close," Gomez said. "When you are ready to return, there is a small black button in the same location on the other side that will alert me to provide access."

"How . . ." I stopped. "Which cats went down there and when?"

"The felines that you refer to as Tuffs, Notch, Spy, and Maul have been down on four occasions. If you wish to know the dates, times, and duration of their stays, I will be happy to provide Jolene the star-time standard of my commander's race for her to apply Earth conversion rates."

Four times. The cats had been here four times. And that had to have been after Spy was an adult and had chosen a mate, which meant four trips down in the last few weeks. *Devious little four-legged sneaks.* "No. For now, keep this between us two. Also, the cats are forbidden access until and unless I say so."

"I am sorry, Shining. I cannot follow that order. My commander and pilot left orders that the cats are to be allowed access as they choose." Along with a peppermint scent from the air filters, an unpronounceable noise came across Gomez's speakers that sorta sounded like, "Garrouling PopPop likes the felines."

The phantom fear increased. "Garrouling PopPop?"

"That is a most unsuitable vocal approximation, without the twelve hertz syllables, and the scent is missing."

"I can't hear or speak twelve hertz, and I can't make smells appear."

"That is unfortunate. Without the proper vocal range and scent, my commander and pilot's name is incorrect."

"So if I meet a Bug alien I should just bow and say hi?"

"Bowing means you are offering yourself as protein."

Bloody hell. Why hadn't I asked this kind of question before? Not that there were any live aliens down there. Just the dead one, so far as I had ever found. Not that I had explored fully in the dark. Once I found the dead Bug, I was done.

Below me, the deck began to lighten and revealed a staircase of sorts, each step with a drop over a meter to the one below, with foot space only half a meter wide, perfect for the Bugs. Not so easy for me. But it was still better than the chute, which had required me to scoot on my butt, palms, and heels. This time, I'd be going down on hands and feet, facing backward, like on a ladder.

I wiped my palms on my pants, grabbed the floor, and dropped over the edge. "I'd like the lights brighter, please," I said as I dropped into the dimness.

The lighting brightened, mostly in the red range, and when my hands pulled away, the hatch closed over my head.

*
*

The ship was built for free-floating, nongravitational travel, constructed of what I'd call interlocking gyroscopes, meaning that lots of things were overhead and/or upside down. I figured that the Bugs didn't need gravity and the gyro let them have access to anything they needed by rotating the ship around them.

I knew what each deck was used for because they were identified by symbols carved into the metal. It was all in Bug language, but on one of my visits I had taken vids of everything, and Mateo and Jolene had later translated from her databanks. I didn't come down here often because it was dark and spooky. I had to admit it was a little less creepy with the better illumination, but not by much.

The ship's power source and engine were located two decks below my office in a metal bubble that was held in place through the center of the ship like the core of a planet. Weapons had to be sandwiched in an outer layer around and between the power source and the command level. When the ship crashed in the junkyard, most of it had been buried by the impact and had rotated so the office was on the top, with windows I could see out of, and weapons unseen. They had to be underground.

I didn't need the engine room. WIMP energies would probably fry me anyway. In desperation, I had once used the ship's shields (which were considered to be weapons, in Bug-think) against Clarisse Warhammer, but I had never been able to make the weapons move using the controls in the Command Chair. Now, I wanted a look at the weapons, if I could figure out where they were located from the inside. In the back of my mind I was curious if the weapons could be powered by an Earth power source, and if I could remove the weapons and retrofit them to take with us, the way Mateo had with the bunker busters. That crazy idea had come to me in the mission-op briefing.

I crawled around the side of the wall along the gyro ring where one of the laser-WIMP-destructor weapons should be mounted—if Jolene's Bug language translations were correct—looking for an access plate. The Bugs would have needed to be able to access the weapon and its mounting at some point, and I figured there would be a way to close off the rest of the ship from atmospheric loss to repair or service things, and therefore I could get to any external weapons from the inside. The first year Mateo and I had come to Smith's Junk and Scrap, we had used a backhoe, digging from the outside, looking for the airlocks and weapons. We never found the weapons from the outside, and I'd never looked for the mounting booms from the inside. I should have. Long ago.

"Could I get some more illumination here?" I asked Gomez.

The light brightened to full spectrum, instantly chasing away most of the creepies.

I crawled, feeling for an access panel. Anywhere. I knew the weapons weren't on top. I'd spent a lot of time up there working on the rain-water collection barrel. No weapons were visible along the sides, or even up to two meters underground, which was as far as Mateo and I had dug out the ground and the bedrock, so they had to be on the bottom half and deeper.

The metal felt fuzzy, scratchy, and slightly uncomfortable to my hands as I worked all the way around the ring, and the ring beside it. There was no discernable access panel. There was also nothing I could identify as metallic nuts and bolts or an attachment plate. When I had worked my way around the rings twice, and was deep underground, I finally discovered a faint groove between the two rings I'd been inspecting.

"Gomez, can you hear me down here?"

"You are within me, therefore, yes."

There was something vaguely insulting and droll about the tone, which I put down to my exhaustion and not the fear that he was sentient like Jolene.

"How are your weapons attached to the gyro? Like plates and nuts and bolts and access panels?"

"My weapons are not attached to the gyroscopic rings. They are part of the rings and develop in place, during the initial growing process."

Growing process? Had to mean manufacturing process; maybe a translation glitch. I ran my hands over the faint seam, where nuts and bolts or the Bug equivalent should indicate where the weapons were attached. There was nothing. It wasn't smooth, but there was the crack. "Where are your weapons located now, in relation to the office?"

"They are beneath me, the weapons rotating into landing struts."

Well *bloody damn*. Why hadn't I asked that to start

with? "So I can't remove them?"

"Only by disassembling my structure at the molecular level or by applying a MAP deconstructing device from the outside. Should you begin a dismantling process, or initiate MAP deconstructing, or attempt to breech my power module, I should be forced to retaliate. I have been equipped with a failsafe self-destruct program. Please do not force me to initiate that program. I like Jolene and wish to continue my research and study with her."

"No! No self-destruct program is necessary." Disgusted with myself, I climbed back to the floor above me and, out of morbid curiosity, opened the panel to the burial room. It wasn't really that—the purpose of the space translated as "Supplies and Health"—but it was where I had found the Bug pilot, at the bottom of the chute I used originally to get down here. The round doorway telescoped open to reveal the empty room. And the dead Bug.

Bugs came in several sizes and shapes. This one was about two-and-a-half meters tall, two meters wide, and was composed of three sections with interlocking exoskeletons. It had seven antennae—three on either end, and one on the center carapace—that together worked as eyes, ears, nose, and probably other senses. They all had multiple limbs, and the scant literature suggested that the number of limbs depended on age and specialization. This one had fourteen.

It had cracked one of its bulbous exoskeleton sections somehow, probably during the battle that had crashed both the *SunStar* and the Bug ship here. It had died. It was still dead, though Gomez always referred to it as "achieving maximum inactivity."

I had never touched it before. Curious, I picked up one of its smaller limbs and considered it in light of the odd knob beneath the command chair. The limb ended in a foot or hand with a central pad and ten small claws around the pad. I pressed on the pad and the claws spread outward, sharp and needle thin. I released the pad and they retracted. I shrugged and dropped the limb, returning to the main area, and closed the oval door behind me.

"Gomez, what did the cats do when they were down here?"

"They explored, much as you are doing. But they seemed most interested in Garrouling PopPop." Again, the smell of peppermint filled the air around me.

"You said your pilot liked the cats. How long after the crash did your pilot die?"

"Garrouling PopPop reached maximum inactivity three of your Earth days after the crash of the ship."

"Did he call his people? Ask for help? No one ever came looking for him."

"Yes. Jolene and I believe that my pilot's distress signal did not work properly."

Or, maybe his people didn't care. Or maybe he was alone on the planet and the signal had to travel to his home world and help was still on the way. Or, or, or.

I started climbing my way out, and gave my shoulders a major workout pulling myself up each step.

I closed the hatch behind me and asked Gomez to air out the office. It stank of peppermint.

*

*

Someone once said that war was hell. They were probably talking about actual battle, with death and maiming and the horrors of people killing people because someone else told them to or to protect what they loved. That said, they likely had no idea of what logistics and transpo might be with Cupcake singing (when we weren't hiding from aerial bots or being tracked overland by dogs and good ol' boys with rifles, at which times she was blessedly silent) and our ATVs strapped to a wartank tracking its way across the excavated stone desert of West Virginia.

It took three nights and two days to get to the bunker. The daytime hours were spent in the elements, hidden by a rare copse of trees and half under the rubble of a disintegrating house, exposed to the elements, with no heat, no AC, no showers, no bodily or mental comforts at all.

The three nights were blacker-and-colder-than-the-pitch-of-hell travel with Cupcake and Amos cuddling (when she wasn't singing), and that was engraved on the back of my eyelids to give me nightmares forever.

One thing was certain. I was never doing this again. Ever.

If I ever found another queen (except Warhammer, who would soon be dead at my hand, or I'd die trying), she was welcome to the world. Screw it. All I wanted was to sleep late, take a bloody damn shower once a week, and eat what I wanted, not run the blasted world.

When we finally arrived at our bivouac, about two klicks from the bunker, I was shaking with misery. The trip could only be described with Pops's style of foul language. So, as I gathered myself to climb down from the ATV at dawn—stinking, wet with sweat, and freezing my butt off— I said into my comms system, "This . . . This was a murderous, pissing hell. You, Mateo, are the son of a motherless goat and a bum-buggering, sodding, rutting pig. If I ever have to ride your rat-arsed Simba again, I'll shoot you with a blaster and laugh as your innards boil. This trip was not just bloody bollocks, it was buggering surgery without sodding anesthesia. I'd rather beat the bishop with a fist full of nails than ever go through this again." My language went downhill after that.

When I was done comparing Mateo's lineage with every disgusting creature I could think of, I jumped the last meter and landed on the ground. My teeth nearly clacked shut on my own tongue, and my knees gave way, as gravity without the Simba's vibration weighed on me. "Son of a goat-buggering-bitch," I said through my teeth.

There was a lengthy silence when I, at last, stopped raging, hanging off the Simba's track, panting.

"Well, I never," Jolene said, sounding all bristly and proper. "You, young lady, are in a foul mood."

"Ya think?" I said.

Mateo, taking his life in his hands, said, "Actually, Shining, there is no physiological way that you can beat the bishop, as that is a male euphemism for mastur—"

"I know what it is!" I shouted, slamming my fist against the Simba's track. "I havta pee, and this time I am not doing it into a cup and then throwing it off the side!" I stomped off into the darkness and found a tree.

When I got back, my team had already begun to unpack the ATVs and the weapons. The cats were running all over, searching for rats or squirrels, as there was some actual tree cover with living evergreen leaves. We had shade.

I collapsed flat to the ground and guzzled a bottle of water before I dragged myself to my feet again and helped my team.

No one spoke to me. No one sang. It was heaven.

*

*

We had been waiting at the rendezvous site since dawn, for the appointed time—which was supposed to be noon. It was now near sunset, and the clubs hadn't shown. A long afternoon of planning and worry, and finally acceptance that they weren't coming.

Spy didn't offer any intel from the clowders of cats with the other bikers, and turned her head away when I asked what she knew. I figured that meant our cohorts and backup in battle had chickened out. I'd accuse them of cowardice when I saw them again, if I lived to tell them anything at all.

Mateo was hell-bent on rescuing Evelyn, no matter what. Without reinforcements, all our plan options were off the table, so we adjusted our strategy accordingly. Our only alternative was auto bombardment of an exterior blast door by the Simba and similar bombardment of another entrance by Mateo in his warbot suit as a diversion, while the rest of us attempted to enter and rescue Evelyn. My small team would be alone.

Still operating the Simba cloaked and shielded, running silent mode, Mateo was positioned two klicks from the bunker at our six, programing its weapons for bombardment. Amos, Cupcake, and I were in armor, full bodily functions introduced—which *totally sucked*—helmets on and faceplates down, standing near the access air duct Spy had used before. We had battle screens and the 3D map of the bunker created by Jolene—visible, interactive, and operational on the upper left edges of the helmet faceplates. When the face shields opened, the screens would rearrange to the edge, still visible. We were standing at a triangle position with me twenty meters ahead in the center, the others behind, Cupcake at my left and Amos at my right.

The airduct covering lay at my war-booted feet, along with a clowder of cats. The leaders, Spy and Maul, were wearing full camera and comms sets on their tac vests. The other cats were fitted with GPS tracking devices on collars so Jolene could find them.

"Jolene. You got the bunker's defensive alarms, cams, and sensors locked down and looped?" She had spent the day copying the intakes and output from every one of the external and internal devices and taking over the security nodes.

"Affirmative. Ready to initiate."

"Initiate," I said.

"Copy that. Looping is in place. I am established inside their systems."

"Okay. No one else is coming—"

"Shining," Mateo interrupted. "My audio sensors are picking up muted bikes."

I stopped.

"I count five Harleys," he said, "all in full combat mode. Jolene has sent them entry coordinates, and they are approaching from the bunker's five o'clock."

Tears gathered in my eyes. All the day's frustration and fury drained away. I had been afraid. Afraid that, once again, the OMW would send me in alone to face a battle and an opponent that was sure to get me killed. And the people I loved.

"Nine more bikes, all in full combat mode, approaching from *four* o'clock," Mateo added. "Jolene has provided them with their entry coordinates as well."

"Update," he said a moment later. "An additional twenty-three bikes, all in full combat mode, are approaching across the dried-out scrub from the bunker's *three* o'clock. And . . ." He gave that weird metallic chuckle. "There are six bikes, all in full combat mode, approaching from *nine* o'clock.

"All riders have checked in with Jolene. She has recognized and ID'd nine Hells Angels, a mixed party of Black Sabbath and Boozefighters, and the OMWs. The group of six are . . ." He stopped, and I heard the muted bikes over the sunset air now. "The group of six have been given your coordinates. They are Old Man Marconi, McQuestion, and Logan Jagger, with Jacopo Marconi, Mina Marconi, and Camilla Mary Gamble at their six. Jagger and the Marconi kids are armored for war." If Mateo could have sounded relieved, he would have. "Spy," he said, "send out your cat clowder members to each of the newly arrived teams."

I opened my face shield and wiped my face. I was not going to meet warriors with tears in my eyes.

"Logan Jagger's small group has just joined with Charles Whip and the presidents of the Boozefighters and the Sabbath. The leaders are moving to your twenty and have signaled that they are to be placed on a dedicated comms channel with . . ." He stopped again and started laughing. Mateo's metallic laugh was always disconcerting, but this time it carried more than a hint of mockery. "With Commander Shining Smith."

I stopped moving. My armor, reacting to my shock, went into hard mode, and I had to disengage the shielding and hard-mode functions in order to actually breathe. *Commander Shining Smith*? *What the* . . . The largest biker clubs in the US were placing themselves under my orders? "No. No way the leaders of biker clubs are putting themselves under the command of a female, made-man or not."

Mateo laughed again. "Privately, Jagger said the leaders initially agreed with the battle plan we sent, but later bitched about who was to lead the advance team, coordinate the actions of the main teams, and have first access to the weapons and the power source. Since your stated objective was to rescue a prisoner, and you have no intent to take any spoils or resources, that makes you a neutral party, Little Girl. They decided you should go in first because of that neutrality and because the first one in was the most likely to die. They also wisely decided that Jolene—who they think is human—and I would coordinate comms, and their warlords would follow your advance team after you have established a secure position."

"Yeah. Let me stand the greatest chance of dying. That sounds more like it."

"Commander Shining Sugah," Jolene said gently on a private channel. "Your suit is registering stress and increased blood pressure."

I laughed, which sounded of tears more than amusement. "Yeah. Stress." I wondered if it was weird that I wanted to talk to a sentient, sapient AI as if she was a counselor or a girlfriend or something. "Jolene, I smell like

a sweating hog, my hair looks like it's been soaked in engine oil, I'm wearing military armor created to die in, and—
Bloody hell. I have no command experience. Why should I
be commander? Even as a token die-first female."

Her voice changed, dropping some of the Southern
drawl. "Eventually, Shining, you'll remember that you
climbed into a Mama-Bot and fought off its Puffers, breaking them to pieces. You'll remember that you killed Perkers, slowbots, repair-bots, and then survived the PRC's
nanobots. And you left the mini-sized nuclear weapon in
place, which killed the Mama-Bot. And you got out alive. All
when you were twelve. You were able to amass a huge
arsenal, which they know but can't prove. You brought
them together. You created all this. All of it. Without you,
there would be nothing here today and Warhammer would
take over the world. Eventually, you'll realize that because
of who you are inside, you are a queen, even without nanobots. Accept the warriors who want to fight at your side,
even if you are a sacrificial lamb."

I wiped my face again and blew out the words,
"Bloody damn. Open the general channel." The ambient
noise changed—an undertone buzz of muted bikes, like
wind in a rainstorm, though I scarcely remembered such a
thing from my youth.

"You are live," Jolene said. "Tap your mic when ready."

I took a breath and let it go. I tapped my mic to the
general channel with my gloved hand. We needed to talk,
make sure we were on the same page, assure each other of
mutual cooperation. But we needed to get the attack under way, too, before Warhammer's defensive systems bypassed Jolene, saw us, and turned their weapons on us. So
while I had to do a commander's speech, I skipped the formalities.

"This is . . . This is Little Girl. I welcome you all to a little bit of hell. You were sent the schematics. Each of you
accepted a level of the bunker to infiltrate and an objective
to secure. You have instructions on how to approach your
assigned entrances, and Jolene will hack the security systems in each teams' location as needed.

"Look around. You each have one or two cats. Let
them go in front of you. They'll warn you of the positions of

land mines and other passive explosive devices. They will also assist you in finding your entrance without setting off alarms.

"The moment my team is in position and the lead cats have the rats in motion as a diversion, Jolene will open access doors. Your cats may know before you do, so watch them. Access doors will stay open for thirty seconds. Get in fast, and get to cover. Then, when instructed, proceed according to the schematic on your Morphons, or for those of you in the new Dragon Scale, on your helmet faceplate readouts.

"I am activating my cats. Spy, Maul. You are a go."

I triggered the screen that was attuned to Spy. She peeled into the air-duct opening and was halfway down the air access shaft in seconds.

"Spy and her mate, Maul, are wearing tac harnesses with comms and cams. The other cats are wearing only GPS devices so Jolene can track them. All the cats were given access to the floor plans, so your cat team can lead you in.

"My team. To me. We are designated as Alpha, and as first humans to go in. We will clear the way for the others. We are entering through the air shaft you should see on your face shields. For the rest of you, to all teams, good luck, bright sun, and try not to come back with your ass on fire."

No one laughed. Those were the last words spoken before the Battle of Mobile. That had been a turning point in the war against the PRC.

A few meters behind, Cupcake waved at me, and she and Amos jogged away. They would be coordinating from the surface. The biker teams on site would cover us while we tried to extract Evelyn.

My team walked through the dry grass to me, armored and armed head to toe—Jagger, Jacopo, Mina, and Camilla. I switched my mic to our private team channel, nodded to them, and said, "I'm taking point, going down the air shaft after the cats. You are to stay on the surface until my okay because there's one nonfunctioning fan in the way, which I'll have to dismantle. The slope is sharp, about thirty degrees, so I'll be on a line, head first. When the fan blade and its cowling are out of the way, I'll secure it and continue down, taking it with me to the next air-shaft junction, where I'll deposit it. At that point I'll okay for you to follow. All security cameras and devices in the shaft have been deactivated or dismantled, but the defenses guarding the other accesses are unknown."

"Won't Warhammer hear us coming down the shaft?" Mina asked into the comms system.

Smiling grimly, I said, "Our team will access with armor on soft setting. As soon as we're inside, the cats are going to provide a distraction and draw the rats into the human-occupied parts of the bunker. It should be quite a show."

They were going to cause enough pandemonium to give me time to free Evelyn. Spy seemed sure she could direct the rats, but then Spy was young and certain she could do anything.

"Once the cats have created some havoc, your assigned access points will open, hopefully without alerting anyone inside, and you'll move to your designated areas. With any luck they'll panic and shoot themselves in their collective asses."

My team laughed. We moved out.

*

*

I secured the high-tensile belaying rope to my armor and activated the Dragon Scale glove that Mateo had programed with a universal, auto-adjusting tool kit, which would fit any size nuts and bolts, both old US and metric.

Just before I ducked in, I glanced back at my team and met Jagger's amused eyes. I shrugged, feeling odd leading others. I had always flown solo, and command did not come easily to me, but I did understand strategic goals and tactical positions. I was, after all, Pops's daughter.

"We've never worked together as a team. I have point. Jagger, you're my number one. Once I get the cowling disconnected, order of descent is me, Mina, Camilla, Jagger, and then Jacopo. Jacopo, if Jagger gets stuck, give him a hard kick or two."

Jacopo's dark eyes sparkled. Jagger grunted.

"If I go down, Mina will use my body and my armor as a shield to address any situation as needed." Mina gave a faint nod. The psychopath would do just that and feel nothing using my dead body. She was very catlike in that regard. The best I could hope from her was that she could keep the others alive.

"If I'm out, whoever is left alive proceeds with the mission. Follow the cats' schematics to the prison level where you will complete Objective One for this team—rescue Captain Evelyn Raymond. The code word for her is 'Mateo.' Hopefully she'll respond to the name and go with you. Objective Two is to kill Warhammer. If you get that far, then clean out the nest and divide the spoils of war according to the agreement."

I switched my mic over to our main channel, so I could hear what Jolene was saying.

"And then y'all best decontaminate all your clothing and weapons and bodies," she said on the general channel. "Remember. You don't have long to clean off the poison before you'll all get sick."

"But once Warhammer is dead," I added, "even if you get sick, you won't be under her command. You should be safe. Let that be the reminder to kill her."

I checked the location of my cat team. They were inside the air shaft, waiting near the grill to the fermentation room. Steadying my warboots on the dirt, setting my armor to super soft and silent mode, I bent into the air duct and let myself slide into the dark, head and one Dragon Scale sleeve first. The shaft was smaller than I thought. I hoped Jagger's shoulders would fit. I laughed softly at the thought of him stuck partway down, Jacopo kicking him. My laughter carried over the open channel. And I felt the collective response of the cats, of Mateo, Cupcake, Amos, and Jagger —my team. My laughter had been unexpected, oddly joyful, and it had steadied all the warriors.

Activating my telescoping helmet and my night-sight filters, I slid fast into the dark.

*
*

The fan cowling narrowed the air shaft into an opening maybe twenty-five centimeters wide. The rats had done a good job of clearing away the filter and mesh protection, and the cats had shoved the fan blades aside, but the screws I had to reach were on the other side of the cowling, so I was mostly working around a blind corner, my hand often close to a rat skeleton tangled into the fan blades. Fortunately, the Dragon Scale glove had a small camera I could activate.

As I worked, I tried not to touch the skeleton, thinking about the lockstep rats Spy and Maul would be facing. The skeleton had been a big-assed rat. Had to have weighed nine kilograms when alive. And its teeth were still razor sharp, long as my little finger. I hated to think about Spy and Maul taking on a rat. Or a bunch of rats.

With the glove's camera and implements, it took me only a few seconds to get the cowling and its frame free. Working in a junkyard for so long had given me proficiency with a variety of tools.

"Cowling is free," I whispered into my mic as I tilted the heavy metal and let it rest across my extended arm. It was in front of me, leading the way down, and I hoped my soft-mode sleeve would keep all the fan's metal parts from banging against the air duct and alerting Warhammer's forces.

I released my belaying rope and slid slowly down, my weapons out of quick reach behind me, now depending on the cats to alert me to impending trouble. The adjoining air duct appeared to my side and I used my boots and the rope to slow my slide. Carefully, I jammed the cowling, fan, and rat skeleton into it.

I reached out to Spy. She and Maul were in full fighting mode, their mental connection completely open. I felt their hunting excitement, nearly quivering with happiness. Saw through their cams into the dimly lit room. No rats were visible. Nothing in the room appeared different from the last time they were here. "Way appears to be open and clear," I said. "Team Alpha, begin descent."

I slid down, moving faster on the sharp slope. More belaying ropes followed me, sliding around on the metal duct, as my human team prepared to descend. I relaxed the pressure of my feet, which had been pressing on the duct walls, and plunged fast.

Just before I reached the opening into the big, dark room, I slowed and stopped. Stuck my fist camera out through the rat-chewed grating and verified what I knew from the cats' cams. The room was empty.

Still in the duct, I gave Spy my attention. "Spy, you two can go ahead. Start your rat hunt."

A sense of pure joy came back to me, and the two cats took off. The rest of her clowder was with the other teams, ready to move in on Spy's command, working as contact points with her mind.

For this part, she and her mate would be alone.

Following on her sense of joy in the hunt was a feeling I couldn't quite interpret, but it was maybe the glory of sunset, the wriggling squiggle of dying prey in her claws, the feel of meat protein in her fangs, the taste of rat blood. Spy was in dedicated killer mode.

They bounded for the first cat objective. The rats.

Again using my tool-kit glove, I removed the grate covering and eased it to the floor. I caught the edge of the ductwork to somersault out of the duct and landed silently. "Access point is clear," I whispered. "Holding position." The fermentation room didn't smell nearly as musty to my human nose as it had to Spy's. The steel tanks showed a thin layer of rust and a lot of dust, and the rat droppings were much heavier than I had expected.

Moments later, Mina landed beside me and to my right. Almost faster than I could follow, she began to quarter the room. Camilla moved to my left. Jagger was slower and louder, but he landed and moved directly in front of me. Jacopo was as silent as a cat, and headed directly toward the doorway we would need to clear into the next room.

Room after room, we cleared our way forward, until we were at the opening to the hallway where Spy first saw the lockstep rats. Here, our timing became tricky because when I inserted my glove cam through a small rat hole, I realized what it really meant for Spy and Maul to successfully attract the rats' attention. The cats were nowhere to be seen, but the hallway was full to overflowing with marching rats. They were leaving thousands of oversized rat pellets and a stink I could smell in the next room.

The only other way out of the room we were in was through a rat hole in the wallboard into another room that was likely a supply closet on the schematic.

While the others watched the rats on their own cams,

I extruded a jigsaw on the universal adjusting tool on my armored glove and cut through the wall—which was nothing but hempfoam insulation and wallboard—to the other side. When I inserted my glove cam, it revealed a storage room for paper products. If there had been rats inside, they had abandoned the room for the rat parade in the hallway. I sawed open the space between metal supports. Mina shoved past me and through.

"Clear," she muttered into comms.

When I got through the hole, she already had a mini-cam on the end of an old-fashioned fiber-optic cable under the door to the hallway. She reeled it in fast. "Rats."

I pressed my glove-saw against the wallboard on the other side of the storage room and we emerged into a tiny utility closet. There were more rats on the other side of the only door, so I cut through the back wall. We came out into an unused, dusty office. The hallway on that side of the complex was free of rats, and Mina was first through, clearing the empty corridor, Jagger on her tail. Camilla followed them, her weapon up and ready to fire. Jacopo edged toward her, covering the white-haired girl and me.

We emerged into a part of the bunker that hadn't been well documented, and we were hell and gone from our own first objective. We opened our helmets, which would have negative repercussions if we ran into people, but it was worth it for the comfort. On the edge of the face shields, just above the sleeve where they retracted, Jolene had posted a possible floor plan that might lead us back to our objectives. Theoretically.

Minutes were passing quickly. We were behind schedule, in the wrong part of the compound, and on the wrong level. On Spy's camera, I saw an image of a stairway jiggling up and down. I realized she was running full-out, up a level. I caught glimpses of Maul's front feet as he raced beside her. On the mic pickup, I heard slithering, sliding, tapping, clicking sounds of hundreds of little rat feet chasing after them. It was rats chasing cats, in a reversal of an eons-long hunt.

"Jolene," I said. "Where are the rats in relation to our twenty and the stockade's twenty?"

"Sadly, not close enough for you to boil the little

beasts. I'm updating your map," Jolene said, "and I'm estimatin' there must be three thousand rats chasing the cats. Should you so order, it would be my personal privilege to play the footage for the two people manning the security screens, and watch them mess their drawers knowing they have to fight them. For now, I've marked a route to the stockade that lets you avoid all the rats."

"Jolene, you share that rat-vid at any time you think you should," I said.

"Oh." There was an odd silence, and I realized that Jolene had just been told she could think and act independently of me without an established protocol in her databanks. I'd just treated her as another human. "Thank you, Commander Shining Sugah. Roger that."

I checked the screen, turned right instead of left, which felt like the wrong way, and spotted a door marked with a staircase. Mina inspected the floor and along the stairs with her tiny camera and pronounced it clear. She eased open the heavy door, and Jagger brushed by me. For such a big man he was light on his feet.

"Security cameras are on rolling blackouts and replay along the marked route," Jolene said. "Hold. There are two humans leaving the upper floor and coming down."

We backed into the lower hallway, let the door close silently, and waited. The others followed my lead when I deployed my helmet. My hands were sweating inside my armored gloves. I didn't want to kill someone who hadn't attacked me, but I might have to. Like the brown-eyed woman. I drew my blaster. Reconsidered and made a fist. Showed it to my team. They nodded, that quick jerky movement of the battlefield or sudden unforeseen violence. I adjusted the anti-recoil settings on my sleeve, and waited.

The door opened.

Jagger took the first one out with a punch that picked the guy up and slammed him into the stairway wall about a meter off the floor.

I clocked the woman, moving in tandem with him. Both of us faster than human.

Camilla stepped back, watching us. Mina and Jacopo covered the stairway as we secured the thralls with military shackles and gags and pulled them into an office. But I knew the three saw the speed, the precision of our movements. That might come back to haunt us later.

Much later, I hoped.

At the next landing, Mina pushed me aside again and took point. Jacopo was at our rear, Camilla beside him. I found myself in a staggered position near Jagger and felt his eyes touch on me and away, as he monitored our progress on the shield screens and ahead, and yet kept track of me too—the hyper-alert focus of an Outlaw Militia Warrior. Or a thrall. Hard to tell the difference.

Over comms, Jolene said, "Don't open the door to this level y'all. The cams are active, and there's fifty million rats out there. That was hyperbole, but there's so many I can't estimate. The security team on shift just saw the rats, and they are clearly not happy people."

We came to a stop. Overhead, a red light began blinking. The red light on a camera at the next landing went dark.

Jolene said, "A general alarm has gone out. A team of Warhammer's thralls has been awakened and called to respond, but they have no idea about the numbers of attacking rats. They are entering the corridor just beyond the stairwell where you are positioned."

"I need to see this," Mina said. She eased open the door a crack and dropped a cam with a mic. Over comms came the sound of a door opening. The scream of humans. Answering screams as the mega-sized rodents encountered Warhammer's panicked thralls. Gunfire rang through the air as the rats attacked anything that smelled of meat.

Jolene put Mina's cam on our face shields. I saw rats in a mound, quivering as they ate something that was still alive, shaking, and screaming.

I could boil the rodents with my blaster and save the humans. My hand closed on the blaster's grip before I released it. The humans had stopped firing. Stopped screaming.

Mina cursed, removed the cam, and closed the door, shaking her head as if to shake off the memories of what she had seen. Seems the psychopath had never seen critters eat humans. Except for the flailing it was pretty much like the way the cats attacked dead humans. Soft tissue first.

Camilla edged closer to Jacopo, the two covering our six, moving carefully up the stairs.

I checked Spy's cam and saw she was close to the stockade. There were no rats there yet. She was ready to create the next distraction we needed to get in and retrieve Evelyn. The plan was for her to push open the door to the bakery, let out a few of the rats she had seen inside that room, and run like her tail was on fire. On the schematic, I saw that all the teams were inside the bunker, moving slowly toward their assigned goals. Jolene was updating everyone about where the rats were, to keep them all safe. Good thing she could multitask. We should have been at the stockade with Evelyn in hand by now. The numbers of rats had been a surprise, and we were falling further and further behind.

We ran up the stairs to the stockade level. Mina checked the hallway and said, "Clear."

"Jolene," I said. "Are there cameras in the bakery?"

"The lights are off, and the cameras there are not multi-spectrum. The lights will turn on when Spy opens the door."

"Shields, helmets, faceplates, and suit hardening," I ordered. "Combat mode." With my left hand, I activated my armor. "Jolene, update."

"Cameras on replay loop with video collected for the last hour," Jolene said, "and Warhammer's security is currently occupied killing thousands of rats. Spy is positioned to create the diversion. I am inside the security node for this level and Evelyn Raymond's cell door is ready to open."

"Spy," I said. "Open the door."

One by one, we exited into the corridor and approached the stockade passage to the right.

"Two humans approaching from the corridor ahead of you."

"Camilla. With me. We've got it," Jagger said. "You three get Evelyn."

On the faceplate screen, I saw the bakery door swing open, the light coming on inside. "Go," I said. We scuttled forward.

On my screen and in my mind, eyes met Spy's. Dozens and dozens of beady black eyes. Fear shot through Spy, lifting her hair on end. She turned and ran.

The bakery door started to swing closed. But there were too many rats racing through. The crush of their bodies held the door open. I saw ten-kilo rats the size of dogs pour across the floor.

The two guards shouted and began to fire.

Shock and fear bled through Spy's connection. Her mind sharpened and focused. She darted the way she had run on the recce. Only to be met by more rats. She whipped her body around. Faced the rats behind her. She was trapped.

"Guards," I said. "Now."

Mina took down the two guards. Gunfire echoing. The guards falling. Attracting the attention of the rats behind Spy. They bounded into the passageway and leaped onto the warm, bleeding flesh. Spy sped five long steps and leaped high. Continuing the run up the wall at an angle, her speed and momentum carrying her halfway up and past the fallen guards.

Evelyn's cell door opened. Spy raced inside. Rats chased her.

"Shut the bakery door," I ordered my team.

Mina and Jacopo advanced into the corridor, firing, wading through rats to close the door.

Maul darted between my feet and into the cell with his mate. Spy sent out a burst of *Save! Fast!*

I ran toward her location. Caught a glimpse of cats in the cell, fighting with two rats, a human behind them, sitting unmoving on a small high bunk.

"Jump!" I shouted.

The cats leaped to the top bunk beside the woman.

I jumped inside and landed where they had stood. Kicked the rats back through the door. Fired at the marauding rats in the hallway. And kept firing when some turned toward me. They charged, teeth bared, tails whipping. Until a second later, their innards boiled. Using short bursts, I swept left and right, my weapon aimed down to avoid hitting anyone outside the cell. Only three mutated rats got past me. Spy and Maul attacked them. Screeching.

In the hallway, my team killed more rats. Burning them. The stench filled the hallway as dozens died. More rats crowded into the cell. I boiled them, but I couldn't take care of Evelyn and also shoot rats. The cats were hissing, fighting, yowling, killing the rats that got past me.

All at once, the rats turned to me. They seemed to understand that I was the leader of their killers. In lockstep, they charged.

Camilla leaped over the pile of dead rats and charging rats into Evelyn's cell and behind me. Jacopo and Mina chose firing angles and blasted away, their killing arcs slowly but effectively cooking rat meat. Camilla and I blasted from inside the cell. The cats jumped back onto the bunk.

"I've got the woman," Camilla said.

She lifted Evelyn into a fireman's carry, keeping one hand free to fire her weapon. I shifted my attention to the cats long enough to make sure they were still ambulatory and not bleeding to death. Then I took a place in the cell doorway and helped boil a path through the rats in the corridor. Jagger appeared at the juncture of the hallway and the cell corridor and picked off rats who made it past Jacopo and Mina.

It was a long, vicious, but one-sided fight. We proved that even mutated rat teeth couldn't bite through armor, though they tried.

When the last rat was cooked dead, nothing moved in the hallway. Rats were piled well over half a meter high. There must have been a thousand of them. Camilla emerged from the cell with Evelyn over her shoulders. Evelyn was emaciated, a corpse-pale body. Limp as a rag doll. No one had needed to shout the code word "Mateo" to gain her cooperation.

Breathing hard, trying not to react to the stench of cooked rats, I said, "Jolene. Team Alpha reporting. Rats down. Objective One secured."

"Condition?" Mateo demanded.

"Alive," Camilla said. "For now."

Jolene said, "Area clear. Security system in the corridor is down, but I can't leave it down for long."

I switched my mic to the general channel and stated, "Team Alpha has acquired Objective One. Report."

"Team Beta reporting," a woman said. "Wingding here. Hospital wing is locked down. Eight medical assistants, one doctor, and three patients are secure. Have left a small team, designation Beta One, in place to cover them. Team Beta Two is proceeding to the food supplies on this level. Have ended four humans. Am alert to the number of rat droppings. Over."

"Team Gamma, reporting. Have entered and secured the vehicle storage and maintenance area and are moving toward the armory." Before his mic muted, gunfire sounded in the distance. Screams sounded closer. "Team Gamma taking heavy fire. Heavy fire! Require assistance. One man down!"

"Team Beta Two, are you in position to back up Team Gamma?" I asked.

"Team Beta Two redirecting. Three reinforcements to Team Gamma. We will be approaching at the enemy's six."

More gunfire sounded. More screams.

"Jolene, did the opposition get word to their security center?"

"Negative. At the first shot, I shut off their comms."

Through the mental connection that Spy had with her clowder, I saw another made-man, this one a woman, fall. The woman writhed on the floor, her body pulled back by a foot and an arm. Gamma was down two fighters.

The watching cat looked at the enemy.

The enemy firing at us wore . . . uniforms.

Of the US military.

I nudged Spy to pass along a careful study of the enemy's clothing.

The cat she was in contact with sped away. Leaped. Vertigo hit me hard at the sideways twist in the air. The cat landed, turned, and studied the enemy, now much closer. The uniforms were not current, but war-time issue. Clarisse Warhammer had put together an army of her own and stuck them in uniforms. I figured eventually she'd just take over the real military from the inside and the make-do uniforms would be unnecessary.

"All teams," I said. "Enemy combatants are wearing US military uniforms from wartime, all branches. Shoot to kill. Repeat. Do *not* hesitate to shoot to kill."

"Team Delta reporting. Have secured the hallway at the entrance to the energy-source room. Instruments indicate no humans have gained access. Door is sealed."

"Team Delta, maintain position," I replied. "Backup delayed."

"Understood. Maintaining position."

"Team Epsilon reportin'," a halfway familiar voice said. "We done secured both ends of the hallway in front of the entrance to the Admin Suite. Awaiting Commander Li'l Girl."

"Bengal?" I asked. "That you leading Team Epsilon?"

"Affirmative, Li'l Girl. Bengal of Team Epsilon reportin' in. You think a coonass member of the Cajun Navy gonna let his number one have all dis fun? Hell, I been shootin' nutria since I a little boy. These military rats is like shooting rats in a barrel and is all de bes' fun I done had in years."

"Confirm," I said. "Rats at your twenty?"

"Only a few hundred. We got it under control. Hey, Puta-Bella. You gots a few at your two o'clock. Fire, damn it. Epsilon out."

Puta-Bella? I shook my head. "Copy that, Epsilon," I said.

"Team Gamma. This is Team Beta Two," Wingding said. "Retreat out of firing range. Beta Two is approaching the enemy combatants from the rear." She paused. "Holy shit. The cats with us just jumped on the enemy. Cats at their heads. Aim low. Aim low. Fire. Fire." A massive barrage of weapons fire sounded, then the odd screaming of the blaster-hit dying. "Commander. Encom down. All eliminated. Permission to assist getting all of our injured to the medical department."

"Make it fast, Wingding," I said, returning my attention to the schematics as we made our way out of the stockade. "Once you have the wounded to the medical ward, assist as backup to secure the entrance to the energy room."

"Team Beta Two, roger that."

"Mina and Camilla. Get Objective One to the air shaft."

"I'm not leaving," Mina said. "I'm staying with the action."

Faster than human, I initiated antirecoil on my suit's nondominant side and whipped to her voice. Picked her up. Threw her across the hallway with my left arm. She crashed into the wall. Her armor went into auto-antirecoil the instant before she hit. Mina had good reflexes. Not as good as mine. But good for a human.

"I repeat. Mina and Camilla. You will obey orders. Get Objective One to the exfil site at the air shaft. Camilla, you will then assist getting Evelyn to safety up the shaft and to the battle tank. Strip her and yourself, then wash her and yourself and your gear. Then re-armor and find me. I'll send a cat to show you the way, if needed. Jolene, open a channel between Mina, me, and you."

"Channel open, Commander Sugah."

I focused on the girl climbing to her feet. "Mina."

Real emotion showed on her face. Embarrassment. Fury.

"You will follow orders, or I will deactivate your suit and you will spend the rest of the battle locked up and unable to move."

Another batch of emotion washed across her face, slower, easier to read. Shock, understanding, recalculation, and retribution. She made sure I saw it all.

I grinned and made sure she saw it. "Yes. I considered betrayal. Yes. Jolene created a back door into the armor function. You will obey orders. Copy?" The little psycho didn't like me laughing at her. I could see her calculating possible responses. A fight between us would be fun, so I rubbed it in a little and said, "You want a fight, Mina? Little Girl will give you one when this is over. For now? I'm your commander. You. *Will*. Obey. Orders. Copy?"

"Copy. *Commander*," she replied.

Her tone was full of vengeance, and I understood that the only reason she hadn't killed me yet was because of a title she didn't think I deserved. That made two of us knowing I didn't deserve to be in charge.

Mina assisted Camilla as she shifted Evelyn in her arms, and helped her adjust her armor's antirecoil and partial, non-combat hardening. Camilla could now carry her burden without effort, and Mina could protect them both. Mina looked at me, calculation hot in her eyes. Adjusting the position of her weapons and drawing a blaster, Mina set it to wide range. She drew another blaster and set it to pinpoint accuracy at six meters. I wondered if she would shoot me, but, without a backward glance, Mina took point, her weapons covering the exfil.

"Open general channel," I said. When Jolene complied, I said, "Mina. Once Objective One is on the way up the air shaft, you will return to our twenty. Jolene will assist if a cat is not available. Copy?"

"Roger that, Commander," Mina said, nothing of her previous emotions in her tone.

"Jagger, Jacopo, and I will join the team at the entrance to the nest, as laid out for the Op. Spy?" I looked at the cat. She was bleeding from bite wounds to her shoulders and haunches. So was Maul. Spy was standing with a rat in her fangs, and the rat probably weighed twice what she did. "Don't eat that. It's poisoned with nanos. Can you fight?"

Spy took the question as a challenge to her prowess. She dropped the rat and hissed at the insult.

"Good. Call your clowder. We need all the cats at the entrance to the nest. Mateo. Release the Maarsie mini-flyers. Get them down the air shaft before Camilla and Evelyn get there."

"Roger. Maarsies deployed," Mateo said. Maarsies were Mobile Aerial Attack Reconnaissance Swarm-bots. A full battery of the tiny flying weapons had been found in the Simba. Each could deliver poison, gas, or an explosive with pinpoint accuracy.

I gave my team the *Move out* hand signal, and took point at the left of the hallway. Jacopo was at our six and to the left. Jagger took position between us, to our right, in a staggered line that allowed either one to shoot ahead or behind without hitting each other or, hopefully, me. We headed out, shooting stray rats as we went. The cats were in front, leading us.

Some minutes later, Mina stated that she was heading back to join her team, trailing a cat. She sounded mildly amused. I wondered if a cat would be a good pet for Mina, soothing her, giving her something to love, or if she would kill the cat. I was betting on the latter possibility.

The cats rounded a corner, whipped back, and raced toward us. Rats lock-stepped down the hallway after them. The cats leaped to my shoulders, claws digging in. I tapped my suit, raising scales for footholds. Mateo and Jacopo moved in front of us and opened blaster fire, boiling the rats alive.

Spy and Maul watched the action avidly. I was glad they didn't have fingers to pull blaster triggers. But then, cats had uncanny abilities to figure things out. Someday they might even steal a blaster. I should keep watch for missing weapons.

We shot rats for far too long.

Mateo said, "Objective One is confirmed safe at the top of the air shaft. Repeat. Objective One is confirmed safe. Camilla is returning with a contingent of cats, including Notch."

Notch was Tuffs's mate and the number-one fighter cat. I hadn't been aware he was with Mateo in the Simba. "Nobody tells me anything," I muttered—and blasted three mega-sized rats in an open doorway behind us. They twitched and died, their little rat eyes on me.

The cats dropped to the floor. I figured that meant there were no more rats nearby.

"Mateo," I said, "Maarsie ETA to the nest?"

"ETA is three mikes unless they encounter resistance."

"Three minutes confirmed," I said.

The plan was to get the door to Clarisse's nest open so that one small group of Maarsies and cats could recon, looking for Warhammer's warriors and weaponry inside. The Simba and its warbot commander would stay in hiding unless or until we needed it, because Warhammer had thralls in the military, and the military would react in force if they knew about a warbot and a battle tank.

"Team Beta Two reporting. Injured are at the medical ward. ETA to energy room, three mikes."

"Team Alpha is on the way to the Admin Suites, henceforth called the nest," I said. "Team Epsilon, your reinforcements will be at the nest in three minutes. As your backup is fewer in number than planned, there will be additional cats and airborne support." Letting humor into my voice, I added, "Do not shoot your backup."

A laughing voice said, "Ten-four on dat Commander. Awaitin' backup, we is."

We moved through the hallways, weapons at ready-to-fire position. Midway along the stairwell to the next level we came under heavy weapons fire from behind. Our armor hardened to combat defensive on impact, leaving us with a full second of immobility before we were able to respond.

In the first half second, we were hit dozens of times each.

My brain and body sped up as adrenaline shocked into me. There were three humans in the rear camera. Mixed uniforms. In the second half second, somehow, Jacopo was able to pivot and return fire with his wide-range blaster. He moved with eerie, emotionless concentration, a ballet of violence.

The attackers seemed to be expecting blaster fire and in the next second, ducked back around the landing and through the door there. Only one was hit, her arm scorched. Screaming.

There wasn't time to clear each floor, not while getting this job done in the time frame allowed—before Jolene missed an outgoing distress call and the military commanders controlled by Warhammer could move in and try to retake their bunker. Every second Warhammer lived, our taking heavy fire was a greater possibility.

My suit unlocked, still hardened, but responding to my need to move. I followed Jagger up one flight, glanced at Jacopo to cover the stairwell, and covered Jagger as he bashed through the door, splinters flying. He exited, firing. A woman screamed.

I saw, in that weird slowed-down reaction to battle, Jagger taking two rounds. I ducked under his elbow and fired from down low. Killed the man with her. Or, we did it together. Two rounds from Jagger and a full blaster from me. He was twice dead. The woman was dead too, lying beneath the man. As I watched, her arm rolled to the side and ripped off, where Jacopo's blaster had wounded her.

I heard a sound from below. Started to swivel. Jacopo fired, wide range with one blaster, and needlepoint accurate with the other.

"Multiple assailants," Jacopo said, his voice steady and soft.

I dropped to him, landing, and added single bursts to Jacopo's wide-range side.

Jagger, directly behind me, fired toward Jacopo. Missing him by a centimeter. Hitting the man targeting him from the open doorway. The man had two neat round holes, forehead and to the right of his nose.

I was breathing heavy. Shaking. My armor informed me it was shooting protein, minerals, and sugar into my bloodstream and increasing the oxygen levels in my helmet. Thinking we were done, I almost told it to stop, but a swarm of rats raced through the broken stairwell door toward us. I swung around and opened fire with my blaster set on wide range, saving the ammo in my handguns. Jacopo danced to the side, taking individual shots with his target pistol, picking off the last of the human stragglers. Jagger crouched against the wall, covering the hall and stairwell on that end.

More rats died.

Bengal was right. It was easy shooting. The rats were being mind-controlled and the rat queen couldn't divide or separate her attention when her teams got into trouble.

Jolene had estimated that there were thousands of rats. I had a mental image of the countryside infested by them, and hoped she wasn't guessing on the low side. To be smart we probably needed to kill the rat queen ourselves, and not assume the bunker busters would take her out. But I had no idea how one might recognize a rat queen.

I tapped my mic to Spy and laid out the problem to her. As I talked, she walked through another open doorway, her odd eyes meeting mine.

Cats didn't have to roll their eyes. They conveyed insult and annoyance with their entire bodies. When I stopped talking, she said, *"Baaaahr,"* which meant, *This place is ours.* *"Mrow. Siss haah,"* she added. *Mrow Siss* meant *dangerous invaders. Haah* was the sound that meant the junkyard cats—Tuffs's cats. So . . . *Tuffs's cats are the dangerous invaders. This place is ours.*

"So you knew that? And you plan to kill all the rats so they can't come back and then . . ." Further realization dawned. "Bloody hell. You planned to set up a secondary command center here? Away from the junkyard?"

Spy stared at me, her tail straight up, her ears perked. The tip of her tail went back and forth. Then she showed me her fangs.

"Fine. I'm not arguing. But two things: you really shouldn't eat the rats unless the queen is dead and burned to a crisp, and Mateo is planning on using bunker busters, so there won't be anything left for you to take over."

Spy gave a chuff-puff of sound that meant *You are disgusting and also maybe stupid*, followed by the equivalent of an unconcerned cat shrug by turning her head away, showing she was bored by the discussion.

Over the general channel, still playing out on comms, I heard Mina say, "Rejoining Team Alpha."

Shaking my head, I hit the mic back to general channel. "Welcome back, Mina. Take point. Shoot to kill rats and any humans in military uniforms. We are following Spy and Maul."

The other teams were taking out rats, and the rat parties were smaller and less organized than the earlier attacks. Progress was slower than I wanted but better than the worst-case scenario. With Mina back, we were nearly a full complement of warriors as we approached the nest. I'd take it.

Behind me I heard a faint whirr and saw the Maarsies in the cameras that gave me eyes in the back of my head. "Team Epsilon," I said. "We are coming up on your six from the stairwell. Once again, I'd appreciate if you don't fire on us."

We stepped over a huge pile of boiled rats and into the hallway in front of the nest. The area where we'd have to set up was empty of rats, dead or alive, but there were dead humans stacked near a doorway, one with a security camera trained on it. The camera was a stationary one and seemed to be still active, though I thought Jolene had taken them all offline.

Spy and Maul ran to the pile of bodies, leaped to the top, and sprayed, their stinky urine marking the bodies as their territory. Then Spy started eating the lips off a human.

"Jolene?" I asked, shaking my head at the cats. "Is the camera system active?"

"They wasn't all stupid, Shining Sugah. They had them some techie types, and seven seconds ago, they managed to seal off parts of the internal security system and switch some of the cameras back on. The energy room and three weapons-rooms cameras are live, so she knows how many warriors guard them. And the cameras in the hallway where you are. I am tryin' to isolate the changes and—"

I interrupted her. "Jacopo. Take out the cameras on this hallway."

The boy—young man—pulled what looked like a twenty-two and fired three shots, shattering three cameras.

"Nice shootin', boy," Bengal said, swaggering out of a second doorway.

I flashed a hand, acknowledging him, and said, "Jolene, advise all teams to take out the cameras on the floors where they're positioned. And then along the hallways nearby. Let's not give Warhammer any assistance."

"Copy that, Sugah."

"You got the plastic explosives?" I asked Bengal.

He hefted a bag and asked, "Where you get this stuff, Li'l Girl? This's primo stuff."

"Warhammer's people applied it to my door when she attacked me. I killed them before they could detonate. Then I repacked it. Waste not, want not."

"My mawmaw used to say dat same thing, she did." He scratched his chin, his faceplate shoved back and open, showing his dark-skinned face. "I used to laugh at her 'cause she save paper plates and plastic cups, and reuse them. Now we don' got no paper plates and no plastic. Yo' cats, they got the 'waste not' idea too, eatin' they enemies."

I flicked a look at the cats and back to Bengal. "Well?"

He gave me a grin I trusted not at all. "I already put what we needed on the door. I think to myself that I keep this extra. Just in case." He pressed the bag against his armor. The Dragon Scale rolled out and accepted the bag, securing it with hemplaz loops at his hip.

I knew what this was. It was the first part of the treachery I had been expecting. Testing the waters. If I let him get away with it, it was a sign I was weak. I also knew I had to do this in a hurry, and in such a way that he didn't lose face in front of his made-men. I hadn't wanted to advertise Jolene's control over the suits to everyone, but since Mina knew, it was only a matter of time before they all knew.

I opened my face shield and walked over, smiling, and was vaguely amused when his face tightened. Bengal was brawny and strong, but I'd been using my armor longer than he had used his. I activated parts of my Dragon Scale hardening and antirecoil. I gripped the neck opening of his suit and tugged him to me, slowly, my suit making me stronger than he was. He bent to me and I showed him my sweetest smile. Softly I said, "Jolene. Isolate Bengal's suit. Harden."

Bengal's armor went hard as a rock. His eyes went wide and he said one explosive curse word. I tapped the loops, which released, depositing the bag into my hand.

I looked inside the bag to verify the malleable plastic explosives were really there. Then, I coiled the bag, and without looking, tossed it to Jagger. My eyes holding Bengal's, I said, very softly, "I'm not badder than you, Bengal, but I'm pretty smart. Now, you can make this look like a big joke, a big game, and redeem yourself in front of the men, or you can act stupid and make me challenge you, and then beat your butt in front of them. Your choice."

"You making an enemy, Li'l Girl."

"We've never been friends, Bengal. And you challenged *me*. You made the first move. I'm not an enemy unless you make me one. Decide. Get beat or keep your dignity?"

Suddenly he laughed. It was a real laugh, as far as I could tell, ringing down the hallways. "You yo daddy's girl through and through. We play this game again, and I be the one winning. How you know I do this thing?"

"You're a biker president. Deceit is axiomatic."

"Lemme go, Li'l Girl. We not friends, but I like you moxie. We good."

I held out a hand to Jagger. "Bag."

He tossed it to me. I put it in Bengal's hand. "Nobody takes from me. But I am very generous. Consider this a gift, the first of many, from Little Girl, to my maybe-someday-friend, Bengal of the Boozefighters. Jolene. Release the suit."

Bengal's suit relaxed, and he threw his arms around me, slapping my back hard enough to bruise, had my armor not been prepared. "Yeah. You Bill's girl. When we gone blow this door open?"

I looked down the hallway. It ended, opening to our right to another hallway guarded by some of Bengal's team. At our left were the sealed doors to the nest, the blast doors that Warhammer had damaged when she first opened them, leaving that crack at the bottom. I looked it over and decided by the scarring and warping, she must have used a rocket.

"Send your team to cover our six and up the stairway and down the next hallway. Then give the order to blow." By letting Bengal give the order to our mixed teams, I was making him my current number one.

He gave the order and shouted, "Positions!"

Our people darted into safety. Bengal picked me up, which I had not expected. He carried me down the hallway, away from the door, shouting, "Fire in de hole! Fire in de hole!"

I started laughing.

The doors closing the nest off from the world exploded.

Bengal tripped. We went down.

My helmet slammed shut as the blast wave hit us.

Smoke billowed out the open doors.

"Son of a bitch, Bengal," I shouted. "How much plastic did you use?"

I swiveled to see the cats and the Maarsies dart inside, cats low, Maarsies high.

Men dressed as soldiers and Marines and pilots came pouring out. Covered in blood. Firing combustion rounds. Everything slowed down as adrenaline shot through me like lightning.

Our made-men in biker garb died in the first onslaught. I could practically see the rounds fly and hit. Their blood in fine droplets in the air. Our suits were battle-mode hardened, us in a pile on the floor. I couldn't adjust my hands to return fire.

It was Jacopo, Mina, Jagger, and Bengal's armored made-man, Puta-Bella, firing from cover, with Bengal and me on the floor in a knot. Six of us in armor against men and women pouring out the exploded door, firing. And then more from the far end of the hallway. They'd had access to the cameras long enough to create a pincer move.

Jacopo directed fire toward the nest. Mina fired over Bengal's head and mine.

My suit unlocked. Bengal's didn't. I shoved my hands free, but couldn't reach my weapons. With my tool glove, I fired a drill-bit into the face of an attacking thrall. Then, two more.

But in two seconds, we were outnumbered.

Jagger dove toward us on his knees. Sliding. Yanked me away from Bengal and shoved us both into a room on the side. Jagger fell against the wall, on one knee. I ripped a flashbang from my armor, shouted, "Flash!" and threw it down the hallway.

Jagger rolled into the doorway across from us. The flashbang went off. Giving us all time to recover. Jagger fired his blaster on wide angle into the smoke. Bengal's suit unlocked.

Bengal and I crawled to the doorway and opened fire. I opted for the blaster. Our enemies had no armor. They staggered out of the flashbang's smoke, screaming, and fell.

"Team Beta Two advancing to take the enemy on the stairs."

In my rear cams, I saw Spy and Maul. They darted out of the nest and into an open doorway. I could feel Spy's panic. Smell the blood on her fur. Sticky on her paws. "Shining, Sugah," Jolene said. "Private channel to you. Spy and Maul were inside long enough for their cameras to show that Clarisse Warhammer is wearing some kind of military armor, and so are some of her people. And she has a barricade midway down the hallway. It looks like the same heavy-duty honeycombed hemplaz carbon-fiber composite that the door is composed of."

"Bloody hell. Someone got intel back to her. Even if it was just last night. How many small rockets or missiles does Mateo have on the Simba?"

"Four SSM antitank missiles that would fit the parameters and goals I perceive you might want addressed, based on the current skirmish as viewed through the armor cams."

"Copy that," I grunted, firing my blaster at a new round of enemy fighters. *How many people did Warhammer transition?*

"Team Beta Two is opening fire."

Screams echoed from the stairwell and down into the hallway.

I slapped the blaster into a charger and pulled an older model Smith & Wesson nine mil.

"Jolene, ask Mateo if he can get in here in his warbot suit and—"

A second wave of fighters poured out of the nest. Firing up the stairs.

"Pull back! Pull back!" someone shouted.

I emptied a mag into a line of advancing thralls on one end of the hallway. Dropped the mag to the floor and popped in another. Emptied it into the attackers on the other end.

"Good shootin' Li'l Girl, but fuck dis," Bengal said. He pressed a place on his armor at his spine and a fully auto machine pistol folded out. I had never seen anything like the weapon. Bengal rammed his blaster into my hand. "Cover our six." He dropped to one knee, supported his body on the wall, and began to fire up the hallway toward the nest. The sound of Bengal's weapon was so loud I couldn't fully dampen it on my helmet speakers.

I dropped flat and began blasting.

Across from us, Jagger and Jacopo laid down fire.

More enemy combatants were coming into my firing zone.

I kicked Bengal's leg and indicated my direction. His new toy took down a couple of dozen, but he went through ammo faster than the speed of sound. Within seconds after he was out, we were hemmed in again on both sides.

I pulled a grenade from my armor. Depressed the striker lever, pulled the pin. Tossed it into the new crowd. "Frag!" I shouted.

Jagger threw another frag up the hallway toward the nest.

We all ducked back as they exploded, seconds apart. Taking out a dozen more encom in both directions. They stopped advancing. Giving us breathing space. Blood, the wounded, and body parts were everywhere.

There was a fine spray of blood across my armor and face shield. The air was full of blood and smoke. I could smell the stench of battle even through the air filters. Gorge rose. I swallowed it down.

The enemy combatants still on their feet withdrew, dragging their downed compatriots into rooms to either side.

Across the hall, Jacopo was on a knee, blasting pinpoint. Took out two who were still moving.

One woman fired from cover. Jacopo returned fire. She died. Methodically, he took down whoever peered out. Jagger did the same in the other direction.

Mina appeared farther down the hall. Fired toward the stairway near the nest, joining the slow attrition of our enemies.

"Jolene," I said. "How many more warriors does Warhammer have?"

"Our people took out the cams, Sugah. But from what I can still access, at least fifty more, coming down from the barracks, various directions. And Sugah, they got bigger weapons. As Mateo would say, big-assed weapons. Some of them are not in my databank."

Bengal changed out magazines. "You a good li'l mofo, ain't you, baby," he muttered to the gun.

I got a good look at the weapon and made sure Jolene did also, through my cam.

"Well, well, well," she said. "Now ain't that interestin'. Warhammer's weapons remind me of Bengal's."

How did Bengal get a weapon like Warhammer's?

"Bengal," I said. "I like your new toy."

"You see dat, eh?" He grinned at me through his face shield. "I shoot a man when we enterin'. I figger I take he gun since he so rude as to bleed all over it. Ain't no way to respect a gun." He held the new weapon out for examination. "Purdy, she is, but a bitch to load."

"I'm glad you got it," I said. I hooked Bengal's blaster to his belt to charge. He tossed me a mag for my nine mil. I replaced the empty in my semiautomatic. "How many of our people are down?" I asked Jolene.

"We've lost six, and seven more injured," she said. "And it looks like what's left of Team Gamma and Team Beta One are taking off with what goodies they can carry. I'd say running like rats, but they ain't in lockstep."

Fifty more coming. Bengal talking to weapons.

"Put me on a dedicated channel to the deserters," I said. When I heard the click, I said, "Teams Gamma and Beta One. If your presidents knew you were running like dogs, they'd shoot you themselves. If you don't return to your positions, you will be hunted down by forces still on the surface." I dropped my tone to a growly pitch and said, "Return to Level One and hold position."

Someone cursed, but Jolene said, "They're finding some courage."

"Good. Ask Mateo if he can get in here in his warbot suit, carrying two small antitank rockets and anything else you two think will clear the hallway leading up to the nest and the hallway on the far side of the blast doors."

"On it, Sugah."

In comms, I heard Mateo and Jolene talking. Then I saw the Simba on a screen inside my helmet, from someone's armor cam. Mateo climbed out of his battle tank like a giant spider. As he sealed the Simba, two of his upper limbs clamped around two rockets.

On open comms, Jolene said, "Teams on the surface. Be aware. The warbot suit is ours. Don't shit your britches."

No one laughed.

Another group of thralls entered the hallway from the stairway where I had thrown the frag. This batch used cover to advance, pushing a steel table on its side in front of them. I fired until the new mag was empty. Messed up the table some. Didn't think I killed any of Warhammer's people. Snapped the weapon into its slot and pulled the slightly recharged blasters. Wondered what a sustained blast would do to the steel table.

"Get in here, Mateo. Make it fast." I fired until one blaster died. The table reddened at the contact spot. I clipped it to recharge at high speed. That would damage the battery, but at this point I'd rather be alive even if I destroyed the weapon.

On our dedicated private channel, Jolene said, "CO Mateo is entering the bunker." She showed me camera view from part of the bunker's security system as Mateo contracted his lower limbs, compressing his height to a little over two meters. Still, his carapace scraped the ceiling.

"Be advised, backup is on the way inside," Jolene said over the general channel. "A warbot suit is entering along the highlighted route on your Morphons and face-shield screens. He also has rounds and fresh power sources for your blasters."

I glanced at the Marconis. They were still firing, but their shots were sporadic. It was clear we were all out of charges and low on ammo.

Jagger met my eyes for a half second. He said, "Pull back until Mateo gets here. Barricades."

I was down to one half-drained blaster. I handed it to Bengal. There wasn't much in the small room to use as a barricade, just a cheap plywood desk and a few plastic chairs. Shoving the desk onto its side, I wedged it at the door. Bengal moved behind it, firing with steady, slow precision.

Amos said, "We're coming in, Shining."

"I told you not to tell her," Cupcake said. "She'll just get mad."

"But we're bringing supplies and ammo, Babycakes."

I actually laughed. "Flashbang!" I shouted. Activated it and tossed it into the hallway. "Don't get dead," I said to Amos and Cupcake. The flashbang went off.

"Who is in position to see into the nest?" I asked on the general channel as Bengal began to reload one of the extended magazines by hand. He'd emptied all he had into the enemy.

Wingding said, "Demetrius, get a look."

"I spy with my little eye, fourteen enemy combatants in the Admin Suite, all in armor," Demetrius replied. "Twelve more in street clothes still standing. And an armored barricade."

"Team Delta on the way," someone said, "bringing ammo and reinforcements to the teams at the nest, but it's gonna take a while. We're having to clear the hallway of rats, both four legged and two legged."

"Copy that," I said.

From the nest, three armored warriors exited, firing. Bengal and I ducked back inside. He slammed the loaded mag home in his borrowed weapon.

"How about you empty that beauty at the armored people up the hall?" I said. "Make some racket. I'm going through." I pointed at the wall to the next room.

"I'm on it, Li'l Girl."

True to his word, he began to fire over the cheap plywood barricade.

I extended the tiny jigsaw on my tool glove and cut through the wall into the next room. It was empty, an office like the one we were in. I crawled to the far wall and made another hole, this one tiny, only big enough to get a cam in. The noise of shooting from inside hid the noise of the saw.

On the other side were three standing humans and a dozen or more dying. I widened the hole enough to fire through. Had just enough charge in my blaster. As the others fired into the hall, I killed them, one after the other. When they were down, I made my hole bigger and crawled through. Everyone was dead. I gathered all the weapons, mags, and ammo I could, passed them through the hole, and pulled a table over to block it. I backed into the room where Bengal still fired, and pulled a table on its side over that hole too. It wouldn't protect us if someone bothered to look, but in a pitched battle, it wasn't likely they would take the time. I gave Bengal three mags for his new weapon, each with some rounds left. He grinned at me like a rich kid on Christmas.

"Mateo?" I asked. "ETA?"

"He's coming down the steps, Sugah," Jolene said. "Amos, Cupcake, and backup warriors from the surface are clearing a corridor on Level Two. All of them have picked up some goodies on the way and are handing them out like beads at Mardi Gras."

Goodies. Weapons. Got it.

On a vest-cam screen, I saw Cupcake mowing down enemy fighters. Jolene accessed another cam and showed me Mateo's longer limbs telescoped up inside, dropping his height so he'd fit into the human-sized stairwell. All around him were dead rats and happy humans, our people changing out ammo and weapons Mateo had lifted off the fighters he'd killed.

Mateo said, "Am in position to fire a rocket into the nest on three. Then in twelve seconds, down the hallway. One."

"Get down," Jolene said. "As Bengal said, fire in the hole."

"Two."

We all dropped.

"Three."

The boom shook the walls and floor. Shrapnel flew.

Dust and smoke filled the corridor.

My head felt the concussive wave from the nest as if I'd climbed a mountain in seconds. I started to get to my feet, and Bengal laid an arm over my back. In moments there was a second boom, this one much closer. I'm pretty sure I screamed.

Bengal and I struggled to our feet. I worked my jaw, trying to pop my ears.

The world was oddly silent. Muted. Muffled.

Jolene said, "Armored enemy reinforcements are moving down stairways toward the nest. Defensive positions. Make ready to fire."

Mateo scuttled down our corridor, pausing at each doorway, dropping off weapons from the dead along with their unused ammo. He looked at me as he dropped two fully charged blasters into my hand and released a bag of ammo to the floor. Maarsies flew around his head.

"Various calibers," he said, "though I see you have some of the new stuff. I'll clear your six again and come back. We can take the nest together."

The warbot lumbered on down the hall. When he reached the end, one of his three short limbs produced a gun barrel and initiated sustained fire for two seconds. Then he trundled partway up the stairs, firing short bursts. There was another massive boom. Mateo tumbled back down the stairs, cursing.

The smoke cleared.

He was missing an arm, wires and cable and bits of metal sticking out of the carapace. Cursing, he opened sustained fire again. "I'll hold them here. Get Warhammer," he said. "Jolene. Take over the Maarsies."

At either end of the hallway, among the dead enemy, I saw Bengal's unarmored people dead on the floor. *My* unarmored people. *Bloody damn*. I should have brought more armor.

We raced, crouched, weapons ready, toward the nest.

Three armored enemy combatants appeared at the nest doorway, crouched, partially hidden behind the bodies of their own people.

I fired, but they didn't go down. From the doorway, more warriors emerged. Our team separated again, seeking cover, and entered doors to either side of the hallway. "Jacopo?" I asked. "There have to be weak points on the armor. Can you hit them?"

Softly, Jacopo said, "Yeehaw, motherfuckers." He stepped into the hall. Extended two weapons in front of him. He fired combustion weapons aimed mid-waist, so fast I couldn't follow his motions. He got lucky, and one of the three armored enemy went down. The others ducked back.

Spy and Maul raced along the hallway with the last batch of Maarsies above them. The cats leaped over the pile of bodies and into the nest. The Maarsies flew along their trail.

Bengal, Jacopo, Jagger, and I raced after. Firing. I caught a glimpse of Mina splayed out on the floor a meter inside the room she had entered. After we passed, my brain registered what I'd seen. She was alive, but her armor had begun med-procedures, pneumatic compression on both legs. She was holding a weapon pointed at the door. She looked pissed. She also looked ready to fire.

The cats and the Maarsies had disappeared.

The two enemy warriors reappeared, firing, this time hidden behind the pile of bodies.

Right-handed, I drew a new forty-four that Mateo had just gifted me and returned fire. Jagger, Jacopo, and I advanced on the enemy warriors. Bengal covered our six and fired down the hall. But we had to duck back into the rooms to the sides. We'd all taken hits. We couldn't keep this up.

I said, "To all backup teams currently making way to the nest doors, be advised that we are under attack from armored warriors. What is your ETA?"

"Team Gamma on the stairs at the far end of the hallway from your current twenty," Wingding said. "Attention warbot. Mixed teams entering the engagement arena. Don't shoot what's left of us." A moment later she added, "Warbot and Mixed Gamma Beta are engaging the enemy. Hot damn!"

Gunshots sounded. Full automatic weapons fire.

"Team Beta Two is coming down the stairs nearest the nest."

Jacopo caught a second lucky shot and took down another armored enemy. Then a third.

Okay. Skill. Not luck.

"Good shootin', kid," Bengal said. "Outta my way. I'm going in."

Bengal engaged his recoil-anti-recoil and leaped over the pile of bodies.

His suit jerked in midair. A piece blew past me. Blood, bone, and shrapnel smacked my right side.

Jagger caught Bengal's body as he fell. He pressed the armor buttons to compress the stump where Bengal's arm had been. Handed him to a made-man with Sabbath patches. Jagger shouted, "Take Bengal and Mina to a med-bay."

Fury whipped into me. They had hurt Bengal. I picked up the weapon he had taken from a dead man and leaped over the pile of bodies. Firing. Controlled bursts. Smoke and debris and body parts were everywhere from Mateo's rocket.

A twisted length of steel had ricocheted. Dropped from overhead to a stop in the nest. The last of the blast dust peppered down.

Jagger entered the nest on my six and took a position to my side and back ten feet.

Down the hall, near the twisted steel, I caught a flash of motion. My flesh buzzed with reaction before I even processed what I was seeing.

Clarisse Warhammer.

Armored. With a curved combat blast shield in one hand.

I glared into her weird orange eyes. "You killed Harlan," I said. "You killed my friend."

Her teeth bared. She raced at me. Screaming. "I will take you. You are *mine*."

I *felt* her attack in my bones.

Standing in a doorway, I fired, full auto, the weapon heating up. The mag emptied. Faster than any human, I dropped the gun on its strap and threw a frag. Caught the gun, replaced the mag, and fired full auto again.

My overheated gun jammed.

Clarisse ducked into a side room.

I turned the weapon off and worked the manual lever, trying to clear it, but I didn't know the specs of the bloody thing. I banged it against the door jamb. I paused long enough to initiate my suit's *clean* function, removing blood and other crap from my face shield.

I maneuvered so I could see Warhammer's previous position through a crack in the door. Her angle of fire was too sharp to do me much damage. I had a sec or two.

Figuring it was useless to me now anyway, I banged the gun again. The shrapnel from the frags was still settling.

As I worked, hands and fingers flying, Warhammer stepped back into the hallway. Shouted through her amplified suit speakers. "I will own you!"

She tapped her Dragon Scale armor off one hand. Tucked the sleeve into her utility belt. Reached out her fingers and scraped them across the length of twisted steel, hard enough to bleed. The blood meant she intended to transition me. "I will take your soul. I will give you to my men. I'll tie you down and cut you. I'll rip you apart—"

"Blah-blah. That's the best you got?" I interrupted. "Evil villain shit?"

"Oh Shining, Sugah. Don't be tickling the devil," Jolene murmured.

With one hand, faster than humanly possible, Warhammer reached through the blast dust into an open doorway. Yanked something to herself.

Jacopo.

Helmet off. Head lolling. Fresh blood smeared and trailing over his face.

She met my eyes. Smiled. "We will not tolerate lesser versions of us," Warhammer said.

For an instant, when I listened to her words from a queen's point of view, she nearly—not quite, but nearly—made sense. And that sent a shiver down my spine.

Queens were built for conquest.

"There will be no other monarchs," she said, placing her bleeding fingers against Jacopo's torn forehead, "for I am sovereign. I will reign over all. You will be mine. Your people will be mine. And you will die by my hand."

Jagger stepped into the opening where the blast doors had once stood. I felt his intent, so I whacked the gun again. Something clicked. I stepped into the doorway to draw Warhammer's attention.

Jagger initiated a three burst at her butt.

She flinched, squealed, then shouted, "Now!"

She bent and leaped. Her armor contracted and released, throwing her body and Jacopo's into the next room. As she moved, something tickled at the back of my brain.

An instant before a rocket launched, I threw myself into the nearest room, rolled behind a bed. Jagger reacted too. I felt his connection to me sever as a blast wave hit.

The rocket destroyed the stairs at the end of the hallway, on the other side of the blast door. Taking out all our backup there. *All our people. Wingding* . . . "Bloody hell," I ground out as shrapnel, debris, and smoke blew everywhere. I removed a jammed round and inserted a new mag in Bengal's toy. Smacked it home.

I stepped into the hallway and met Warhammer's crazed eyes again. Jacopo wasn't with her. She fired. Full auto. I whipped away. The bitch laughed and leaped back into the room across and down from me.

"Jagger?" I asked.

"I'm fine."

He wasn't. I could tell. But he was alive.

The cats dove into the room at me and pressed close to my calves, shaking with exhaustion and fear. I offered each a single stroke. Poured water for them both, which they practically attacked. It wasn't enough for what cats under stress needed, but it would have to do.

"Jolene, are you inside any cams anywhere? And by the way. Bengal's new gun sucks."

Jolene said, "Heat signatures and the cats' vest cams suggest that the enemy combatant's commander, Clarisse Warhammer, and nine warriors have gathered in a small room at the back of the nest. It's possible that there is an emergency stairwell at the end of the hall, and that they are attempting to escape under cover of the barrage."

Jagger said, "You take Warhammer. I'll make sure Jacopo is taken to a med-bay and follow."

"Roger that," I replied. "Jolene. Extrapolate. If there is an exit from the room Warhammer is in, where would she come out and is that outside exit covered?"

"Two of the Boozefighter made-men are at the most likely exit."

"Two against ten," I said. "They'll be slaughtered. Tell them to retreat fast, into cover. And tell them to watch which way Warhammer goes."

"Copy that, Commander." The sentient AI relayed the order.

"All teams. I'm following Warhammer." I said.

"I have Jacopo. I'll follow with a support team when possible," Jagger responded.

"I got two men left," Team Beta Two's Wingding reported from the demolished stairs. "We'll cover both your sixes."

Relief shattered through me. I had no idea how they had survived the rocket, but some of our people were still with us. The cats pressed close and I stroked them each again, more for me than them this time.

A barrage of gunfire sounded.

Wingding shouted, "We're taking fire from Level Two. Unable to assist at this time. Requesting backup."

"Puta-Bella here. I'm injured but ambulatory. How can I help?"

Jagger said, "Get Jacopo to a med-bay, PB."

"Roger that. Poor kid."

Sounds of gunfire and pained grunts sounded through comms. Jagger said, "Look around what's left of the wall, Wingding. One of Team Alpha providing backup."

Jagger was going into a hot zone. I shoved that deep inside where I didn't have to acknowledge it. Not now.

Jolene said, "Commander, I have visual confirmation that Warhammer and nine armored warriors are evacuating up a narrow stairway, out through one of the garage blast doors. I'm inside the cameras systems, but someone, somewhere, is attempting to shut me out. Maarsies are following Warhammer at distance, giving me secondary cam footage."

I dropped to one knee and took in an angle of the hall.

Hidden by the smoke and blood spray in the air, Spy and Maul raced out and through the debris. Following Warhammer.

Run, I thought at Spy. *Follow Warhammer. Be safe.*

"Copy that, Jolene," I said, aloud. "Mateo, are you ambulatory?"

"Affirmative. Exiting the building up a lateral stairway and will approach overland. ETA to estimated exit point, six mikes."

Six minutes. I could last six minutes. I wouldn't be alone.

"Okay, Mateo. Let's hunt down and kill us a Warhammer."

My armor injected me again with meds, sugar, nutrients, and fluids. I had a spurt of nausea as my blood sugar and protein levels upped too fast. A tiny readout appeared, telling me I was nearly out of the good stuff. I got a deep breath as the oxygen levels in the helmet went up too. Six mikes. Until then, that left the cats, the Maarsies, and me to chase Warhammer.

I stood and pulled two new blasters, delivered by Mateo, and said, "Little Girl. Going in. On Warhammer's tail."

I stepped along the hallway, through the smoke. There were bodies—pieces of them, mostly—on the floor where the explosives and rockets had detonated. A small group of unarmored soldiers raised weapons toward me. One tossed a frag. Then another. As they fired and the grenades flew through the air, I ducked into an open doorway. Whirled behind cover. The frags detonated.

I extended one arm into the hall and blasted the three standing there. Instantly, six more began to fire from cover.

I had frags, too.

I pulled and tossed. Ducked back.

My frags detonated. One person started screaming.

My armor readout said my heart rate and blood pressure were too high.

No shit.

There was a door into a bathroom. I raced though and out the other side, into a sitting room, firing. Dropped two more unarmored encom with blaster fire.

Tucking my glove cam out in the hallway, I saw no one standing. Just debris and several deactivated Maarsies. They had expended explosive payloads long before Warhammer's rocket.

I adjusted my view. There was a lot of blood. Everywhere.

And a dead cat. It had been shot.

Damn it.

It wasn't Spy or Maul, but a skinny tabby. Still. *Bloody damn.* Altering my glove's angle, I checked out the entrance of the Admin Suites. There were four of Warhammer's fighters still firing out into the hallway at the last of our people, their backs to me. I finished them off and eased out.

I trotted down the corridor, moving slowly, clearing each room.

"I'm through. Nest is clear," I said. I checked my faceplate screen to see the vid from Spy's and Maul's vest cams. They were on the move, running up some stairs. "I repeat. All enemy combatants in the nest are down. Jolene, show me the cats' location on an interactive map of the bunker. And the Maarsie locations."

New schematics and 3D floor plans appeared on my screen. I could see Spy and Maul on the move, brightly colored dots. The Maarsies were blotches of green. "Jolene, you're monitoring this. Did you spot any traps made or being laid? Any place where humans are waiting?"

"Negative, Commander," Jolene said. "All teams on the surface, be advised. CO Mateo is traveling to Warhammer's apparent exit point. He is on the surface, in his warbot suit, running concealed. Shining," she said to me privately. "Objective One is in a med-bay in the Simba, sedated, undergoing treatment."

Mateo had protected Evelyn. He was either coming to get vengeance on Warhammer for what she had done to Evelyn, or he was coming to back me up. Either way meant a better chance of achieving Objective Two: Clarisse Warhammer dead.

I had a sudden vision of Harlan, dead at Warhammer's hand. Tortured. Eaten by bicolor ants. I wanted to kill her slowly, but as long as she was dead, confirmed dead, and I got to see her dead, I was gonna let that count.

"I should be heading out in seconds. Tell Mateo not to shoot me."

I tore into the tiny room and up the stairs.

Jolene said, "Warhammer's exit point is marked. Six mini-tanks are exfiling the scene." On my screen I saw a cluster of blue dots. *Warhammer*. Her route was marked in yellow. I raced to follow across an unlit landing, up two flights of stairs, and into a cavernous space. It was full of military mini-tanks and armored and weaponed all-terrain vehicles. The garage we had seen on the initial recee.

I turned on the armor's speed function and dashed across the huge room. There was an empty area with fresh, oily looking droplets of hydraulic fluid and liquid fuel on the floor. From outside I heard weapons fire. Who was shooting at whom? Had Warhammer's fighters been ambushed?

"Jolene. Please advise the following: Who is firing? Are all of Warhammer's unit still with her? And what can you tell me about their vehicles and weapons?"

"Warhammer and all nine fighters are firing into the brush as they travel, on six armored mini-tanks. To this point, none of our remaining on-ground forces have been injured, but there are only a handful that didn't join the bunker battle.

"Warhammer's unit is carrying the same model of weapon used in the bunker, and they seem to be carrying sufficient ammunition to fight a protracted battle. They have no missiles or rockets. There are confirmed visuals of two cases of fragmentation grenades. Repeat. Two cases. Spy and Maul are with her team, together, with a third cat, on the back of one of the mini-tanks."

"Dang cats."

"Be advised, Commander, that Warhammer and her personal defenders are all wearing armor. It appears to be first-gen Dragon Scale auto-hardening war-era armor, model DSAH10. This model has fewer high-tech modifications and more specific weak points than your model. However, DSAH10 is capable of withstanding small arms and hand-held blaster fire."

I raced through a massive garage door and down a wide hallway. Then up the ramp toward the night where a set of blast doors to the outside had been left open. The stench of exhaust registered strong on the air.

I remembered Jacopo's "Yeehaw, motherfuckers" and I laughed, the sound a little crazed.

It looked as if it was going to be a few cats, a warbot, and Little Girl against ten fighters and six tanks. Could be worse.

"Jolene, relay orders that all teams are to get our in-jured people to the bunker's medical facilities, clear the building room by room, and take the gear and supplies each club agreed would be theirs." I dashed outside, fol-lowing the ATV tank tracks. "Notify everyone that—" I stopped. *Bengal injured. Maybe dead. Mina ditto. Jacopo in a med-bay, hopefully. I want Jagger with me, but that isn't where he can do the most good.* "All teams. Logan Jagger has command until I get back."

"The fuck you say?" Jagger said.

"Jolene, if he tries to follow me, harden his armor."

"No!"

"Roger that, Commander," Jolene said.

"Little Girl has left the building."

*

*

The tanks had moved fast. I needed speed and increased the armor's assistance to run. Initiated the gyro properties for when I mis-stepped or started to fall. Decreased the suit hardening so I could breathe deeper. Punched the but-tons for another blast of oxygen in the helmet. Switched blasters for long-distance pinpoint accuracy and auto tar-geting with IR and lowlight assistance. Because somehow it was still nighttime.

I practically flew, following three Maarsies' locations on my screens. The tanks were a half mile ahead and mov-ing fast.

"Mateo here," his metallic voice said. "I have Little Girl in my sights. Coming up on your four o'clock, one klick out." I glanced in that direction and spotted trees on the bunker hillock waving against the night sky as my seven-and-a-half-meter-tall sidekick raced in from my rear. His warbot suit was in full invisi-mode and likely using all six limbs, including the stumps of the amputated and dam-aged ones, to knock dead branches out of his way, to catch up to me. Good thing I wasn't scared of spiders.

I raced down a dry creek bed and across bare stone. Up a hillock.

"Shining," Mateo said. "Shooter coming up on your two o'clock. In a tree. I'm too far out to hit him without using explosive weaponry which would be heard by War-hammer's team."

I slowed and ducked behind a dead tree, scanning the area Mateo described. I spotted an armored man sitting about six meters in the air, his legs wrapped around a tree, hardened to its trunk.

I wasn't nearly the shot Jacopo was. *Not good.*

I rested the butt of my only fully charged blaster on a stub of a tree limb and studied his suit. I wasn't familiar with this older model. "Jolene. Describe First Gen DSAH10 military armor."

"DSAH10 military armor presents—"

"Design flaws and weaknesses," I interrupted.

"Air filters have minimal shielding. Weaknesses also exist at the seams beneath arms and at the groin. Maximum damage may be achieved by sustained heat, lasers, or blaster fire, and by projectile weapons larger than nine-millimeter caliber rounds fired at close range." Jolene sounded stiff and cold as she told me how to kill.

The shooter's sitting position meant the seams were out. "Air filters," I muttered. "Jacopo could probably hit them with both arms tied behind his back." I auto-targeted, took a breath, and let three-fourths of it out.

I fired.

The blaster took five seconds to melt through the filter and damage the suit, and an additional two seconds to hit the man.

Bloody liquid splattered onto his face shield.

His head rolled back.

Mateo appeared behind me, faint whirrs and clicks the only sound, visible only now that he was close. "Nice shooting," he said. "Try to keep up." He was missing one entire short limb and another was damaged, metallic bits and cables dangling as he tore after Warhammer's tracks.

I laughed softly and followed. My suit injected me with the last of the liquid, hormones, 'roids, and supplements. I'd be hyper and unable to sleep for a week.

Jolene said, "The cats with Warhammer are no longer progressing. They are at the remains of a building to your ten o'clock. Their vest cams have two humans in sight. It's an ambush."

Mateo veered right, then back in a zigzag motion. I went left and watched as he came around in front of the pile of rubble, his enviro camo vanishing. The sudden appearance of a nearly three-story tall spider gave him the moment of surprise he needed. He scooped up both snipers and threw them to the ground. Then tossed them high, caught them, and bashed them onto the rubble so fast, so hard, their armor buckled and cracked open. "Finish them," he said to me.

I killed a female sniper in her cracked armor. The other might have been male. It was hard to tell. I shot him too. Three cats eased out of the building wreckage and surrounded me. They looked exhausted and thirsty. Spy leaped to my thigh and tried to hang onto my armor. I picked her up, put her on my shoulder, and tapped two pieces of shoulder scale. They lifted, just right for two of Spy's four legs. Her claws came out and she gripped them.

She nudged me to look at Maul. The cat was bleeding, breathing fast. He couldn't travel, not now. But he was still alert.

"Maul," I said. "You and your other clowder cat—" I stopped when I recognized Notch. He was bleeding too. *Bloody damn.* "You and Notch stay here. We need you to keep your camera trained on this path. If other enemies come, that will let us know."

Maul showed me fangs, then turned his head away. Notch sat down. I figured that was the only agreement I was going to get.

"Hang tight," I said to Spy.

I sped after Mateo. Caught up with him in less than a minute. Side by side, the three of us chased the mini-tank tracks.

"According to the Maarsie cameras," Jolene said, "there is a military convoy two klicks away."

"Bloody hell. We can't catch a break." I was already running full-out, at the best speed the suit could give me. Mateo was taking easy strides, staying with me. In the distance, I heard the sound of the mini-tanks, the roars of the old tank engines at top speed, bouncing on uneven terrain.

Jolene said, "They just took out the Maarsie queen bee. I no longer have visuals."

"I have visual," Mateo said. "See if you can interfere with military communications and redirect the military convoy north, per my order."

"Yes *sir*, CO Mateo," she said, all the Southern gone from her voice, reverting to her *SunStar* starship AI. I realized that Mateo's order might be construed as treason. "CAIT. Obeying orders not in compliance, re: 2045 USSS Articles of War."

At her words, Mateo stopped.

CAIT. Not Jolene. CAIT was the ship's AI designation before she developed sentience.

We had all been skirting the edge of sedition for months, but somehow with his current order, lines had just been drawn, lines that couldn't be un-drawn in time to save us from being charged with treason if we were caught and if CAIT's memory was ever scanned.

"Bloody buggering hell," I said.

"Yes." Mateo aimed. "Enter my orders into ship's log at this date and time, by my orders."

I raced ahead, knowing Mateo would fire over me. I heard nothing, but my faceplate showed me he had fired his lasers, all of them. The sound of engines grinding and failing clanked and whirred in the darkness, telling me he had aimed true.

I rounded another pile of rubble—a hotel, according to the remnants of its sign in my lowlight face-shield screen. I spotted three mini-tanks. One was overturned; another had crashed into it. The third was on its nose, rocking back and forth, trying to right itself. I tucked myself into a crevice behind a broken ancient cement-block wall. Auto-targeted two blasters at the humans I could see, but their heads and air filters were turned away. I fired anyway. Retargeted. Fired. Nothing changed. Their armor was old but solid at this distance and angle. It was going to have to be up close and personal again.

Watching for movement, I said, "Jolene. We've taken down three of Warhammer's warriors. We have three more in sight here. So that leaves Warhammer and three others. Do we have any Maarsies still flying, and can you ping their positions?"

"We have two Maarsies left flying. No cameras. From

their pings I am capable of calculatin' their coordinates, though the mini-tanks will have moved well beyond the Maarsie positions."

"That sucks. Work on that while I clean up here."

The crashed mini-tank engines were hot, which would hide my heat signature on IR and decrease their likelihood of seeing me in lowlight. Two of the warriors were ambulatory and trying to get their buddy free, covering the night with blasters as they worked. Grabbing Spy with one hand to keep her from being slung around, I darted to the closest tank and fired from behind and beneath the tank at the driver. Point-blank at the air filters. The biggest weak point in the old armor. The driver died. I repositioned and fired. One more, then the other, died.

Spy bit my glove to make me let go.

"Sorry," I muttered to her. She hissed at me, showing fangs.

"Jolene. Update. Only three enemy combatants and Warhammer remain active," I said.

Mateo was already ahead of me. I took off after the warbot. For all the discomfort of having initiated the bodily fluids mode on the armor, I was glad I had, because it had been hours since I last peed.

*
*

Half a klick later I came upon three more wrecked minitanks. One driver was dead at the wheel. Mateo, fully visible, was holding another man by one arm, peeling his armor off by brute force. It was One-Eyed Jack, Warhammer's Number One and mate. He was screaming. The sound got worse when Mateo started pulling off the man's fingers.

Clarisse darted out from her overturned tank and fired a three burst at Mateo. It was like shooting at a five-centimeter-thick steel plate. Mateo ignored her and pulled another finger off One-Eyed Jack. The dangling man squealed. Clarisse fired fully automatic, her fancy new weapon bouncing with the action. In seconds she had emptied the extended mag.

Mateo swatted her with a leg. She flew in a tumble of limbs. Rammed hard against a tank track.

I felt the vibration of her landing as if I'd taken the blow myself.

In that fraction of a second, I realized our nanobots were weirdly attuned.

She pivoted and spotted me. I literally felt her eyes on me—invasive, crawly, heated with fury.

I knew her intent even before she raised a blaster. I lifted an arm to block and swiveled so Spy was protected by my helmet and body. The energies bounced off me. Spy dropped from my shoulder into the shadows of night.

I stood. Met her weird eyes across the distance.

"You're about to die, Warhammer. And just for kicks I'm going to tell you why. You could have had anything and everything in the world. But you took Harlan. And so I'm ending you."

Warhammer screamed in mindless rage. She swung the auto-gun around her shoulder on a strap. Caught it. Pointed it at me. But she hadn't changed out mags.

I brought up my own blaster. Auto aimed for the air filter near her left ear. Fired. Steady stream of power.

Warhammer fired. Nothing happened.

My weapon still tracked. Melting a hole at a helmet air filter.

Warhammer ducked behind one of the tanks.

The blaster lost tracking.

From above me somewhere, One-Eyed Jack stopped screaming, now grunting irregular gurgling breaths.

Mateo fired a three burst. I had no idea what he was shooting.

Warhammer stepped out from the mini-tank.

Auto-tracking again, I shot her. My blaster should have boiled her brains, but she shifted, the tracker slipping away again. It was calibrated for human speed. We were faster.

Bloody damn.

She raised her gun.

Warhammer had reloaded.

She fired.

I leaped to the side as she emptied the weapon, wasting ammo.

Behind me, One-Eyed Jack fell silent.

Hidden behind a pile of refuse and debris, I stretched

out low. Steadied my blaster. Aimed at her helmet. Fired again. Missed. Warhammer was as fast as me.

She raced down the deserted street, leaping over debris, skirting behind rubble that had once been buildings. Firing all the way. Then she pulled out a new weapon. I couldn't see what it was. She stopped, turned, aimed at me where I lay in the bricks and rebar. She fired.

It sounded like a cannon going off.

"From your armor cameras," Jolene said, her voice unusually crisp, "I can tell that Warhammer is firing a Smith & Wesson Model 500, once the most powerful handgun on the planet. The bullet diameter is 12.7 millimeters. It is also unsuppressed, Shining Sugah, and the military convoy nearby has heard her weapon fire. They are maneuvering to investigate."

I cursed.

"Sugah," Jolene continued, "do not let that woman fire at you point-blank. You *will* sustain damage."

"Not in my plans."

"Without Maarsies with cams overflyin' I cannot tell you how soon the military will send their own reconnaissance flyers or how soon they may arrive on scene. I am attemptin' to track their communication system, but they seem to be aware of my interference and have put up firewalls of a kind I have not encountered before. You better hurry, Sugah."

I rolled to my knees and moved silently around a bigger pile of rubble, rebar sticking up and out and bent like pretzels. I reset my armor and crawled through a small hole. To the side, Mateo began to dismember Warhammer's last fighter, the screams high-pitched and desperate. He didn't last as long as Jack had, dying in seconds.

My speakers picked up the low scrape of movement just ahead.

It was clear Warhammer's armor had far fewer bells and whistles than mine did. Her soft-mode was loud where it brushed the wreckage. But her body was augmented. Even without the new speed functions, gyros, and mechanical reinforcement, she was fast.

I peeked out from behind an exposed basement foundation.

Mateo reared up over the wreckage of the buildings. "Your turn," he said, his metallic voice echoing through the wreckage.

Warhammer tripped over a low wall. Landed. From the ground, she fired at Mateo with everything she had. Mateo moved slowly toward her, his legs like a massive spider, her rounds bouncing off his carapace. Her gun jammed.

"Peel pieces off you like I did Jack, for what you did to Evelyn."

"She's mine," I whispered to him. I set my blaster on auto-aim, auto-fire. Weapon out in front, Harlan's dead face in my mind like a beacon, I ran for her.

Leaped over the low wall. Engaged auto-targeting.

The barrel end of the biggest handgun I had ever seen was pointing at me.

She had faked me out.

In midair, I tucked, swiveled, pivoted, rolled. The first round caught me ten centimeters to the left of my navel, in the pad of flesh at my waist.

Pain slammed through me like a tidal wave hitting a shore, overriding everything.

I landed wrong. Things broke.

But my hand still worked.

Auto-targeting readjusted.

I fired.

Warhammer's helmet melted at the contact spot. Her face turned scarlet. Her cheeks and nose boiled and melted. Her eyeballs, that disconcerting orange like mine, bulged and burst. Blood and viscera splatted on her face shield.

It wasn't enough. I kept firing.

Inside the helmet, her head . . . exploded.

Skull fragments, blood, and gray matter hit her face shield.

The face shield opened. More of her filth pulsed onto my armor and helmet.

My armor cleaned the gore from my faceplate.

Her neck stump pumped a final gush that fell to a trickle.

Clarisse Warhammer was dead.

I had killed her.

"That worked," Mateo said.

Breathing hard, hurting, I studied the queen. What was left of her.

My suit began sending out alarms. I shut it off. I knew it was bad. I didn't need the list of injuries.

I punched a button on my suit. It stood me upright, and I walked to Clarisse's body and picked up her right hand. Lifted it across her body and with her own index finger pressed the disengage button under her left arm. Her armor opened up like a lobster tail, splitting down the legs, then the arms, then the torso.

Clarisse Warhammer really was dead.

"Harlan," I said aloud. "You are avenged, my friend."

The pain increased. I was breathing too fast.

My suit overrode my commands and broadcast alarms.

Darkness descended over my vision.

My gyros failed. I fell over.

The ground came at me.

*

*

I woke to see a darkened room and a vision of a human face, but elongated like a hologram with bad software problems.

"Jagger," I murmured. "You look like shit."

"I look better than you," he said, a weird stretched-out smile lighting his far-too-pretty face.

"Am I in a med-bay?"

"Yes. In the bunker medical ward. You got hit. Multiple times," he said, conversationally. "Your armor managed to deflect or absorb most of the rounds, but a few things got through."

He was out of his armor, wearing his kutte, a long-sleeved T, and jeans. He looked relaxed and relieved and freshly showered and scrumptious. Sadly, I think I said that to him.

He chuckled and said, "I didn't think Mateo would get you back in time, but he did. He managed to damage another of his remaining short limbs getting you to safety."

"That's going to be a bitch to replace," I said. "Warbot limbs are in short supply."

Jagger smiled slightly. "Fortunately, Jolene was able to override the programs of a med-bay that had been triaging a Sabbath and put you in. We got you stabilized."

"The Sabbath?"

"She lived."

"Okay. What shape am I in?"

Casually, as if he was at a *bloody damn tea party*, he said, "Upper descending colon was hit and was resected. The lower lobe of your right lung was hit. Fracture of your dominant arm in three places when you took fire and then immediately landed wrong. You have titanium plates, rods, assorted screws, and various unpronounceable bits of mechanicals inside you now. Mateo described you as having warbot bones. Your nanobots are healing you at an astonishing rate of speed."

I breathed out a sigh. "Evelyn?"

"Stabilized physically."

Not healing. Just stabilized. That was bad. Those two words said a lot about Evelyn's mental state.

Jagger added, "We didn't think she had been transitioned, but we were wrong. When we tested her with your nano detector, the nanos were at a low level, not high enough to heal her like yours are healing you, but they're present. Mateo said something about transitioning her to heal her fully."

My father's face flashed into my memory. I'd killed Pops when I tried to heal him. "Where is she?"

"Mateo has her in a med-bay in the Simba with him. He's nursing her."

Mateo knew as much about healing with med-bay protocols and Berger chips as I did, and a lot more about protocols for injuries. "Okay. What about the military convoy that was nearby?"

"Mateo hauled most everything off before they got to the kill site. Military found signs of a battle. One body. No armor. Blood, bits of intestines, a finger. Some mini-tank parts. They decided it was local gang warfare and withdrew."

I chuckled, and it freaking hurt. When the spell of pain passed, mostly, I asked, "Bengal, Mina, Jacopo?"

"In that order, being fitted with a replacement limb; in a med-bay with femurs being repaired, and pissed. Warhammer managed to transition Jacopo before she dropped him, so he'll go through med-bay protocols when one comes open."

"What about the rats, any of Warhammer's thralls left alive here, and the WIMP power source?"

"The cats hunted down and found the rat queen. I went in and killed her, and then burned her body. The rats are . . ."

He stopped and scratched his bearded chin. He looked good with a five-day beard, dark and bristly as a porcupine. His pretty eyes met mine. "The rats are sitting in corners, staring off into space. They don't run, eat, or drink. They're dying where they were when their queen died."

I scowled. That wasn't good. If the rats were dying in place because *their* queen died . . . "And Warhammer's thralls? Are they sitting and staring off into space?"

"Yes. At first. There were only twenty-four left. Once our own people were stabilized and the less injured moved out, the thralls were put into med-bays and flushed with fluids, and while they don't seem anywhere near a hundred percent, they do feed themselves and take showers when told to."

How was I supposed to care for that many queenless thralls? "What do the medicals think about any further improvement?"

"Maybe. Slowly. They did better when we took them out of the bunker and let them see sunlight. Most hadn't been outside since they were captured and transitioned."

"The WIMP power source?"

"Untouched. Unfortunately, everyone knows it's there, whatever it is—power source, weapon, or both. Eventually someone will come after it. Mateo and Jolene are prepared to bring down the bunker without damaging it."

"Hmmm." Mateo's bunker busters. Some things were great. Some were not so great. Much like life in general.

"What about Warhammer's nanobots? Is everyone washing appropriately?" Warhammer was dead, but her nanobots would still transition anyone they got on for seventy-two hours.

"The Sabbath rigged up a water line from the bunker's pump to the outside. I issued orders for showers every hour for anyone inside. Clothes are washed and worn wet.

And then showers again in an hour. Nobody's happy, but everyone's following orders. They saw the rats."

"Yeah. That was scary."

Jagger opened the med-bay. Picked up my hand. He traced the bones beneath the surface of my skin. His fingertips felt rough and scratchy. I liked it. "Mateo also said that alarms went off at the junkyard this morning. Wanda called for assistance and then was cut off. Jolene said the office was shaking, and then went silent for two hours. Shit's happening there.

"An hour into her com silence, Mateo took off in the Simba with Evelyn still in a med-bay, running in silent, full combat mode. He said to tell you that you have thirty-six hours before bunker busters kick in."

Mateo must have left them emplaced, aimed, and ready to fire. I had a day and a half to clear the bikers out of the bunker, which I was sure they all wanted to claim and would happily go to war over. *Bloody lovely.*

"Jolene?" I asked.

"Your Jolene came back online twelve minutes ago, demanding we wake you up. I had no idea Southern ladies could sound so pissed."

Jagger held up a finger and tapped his comms. "Anyway, you need to hear what she has to say. Jolene, you're on."

"Just so you know, Sugah, I just shot up a passel of bikers on matte-black bikes carrying the latest in military gear. They were all wearing black unmarked street clothes with no kuttes, no insignia. I am currently tracking the serial numbers of the ruined bikes, and Wanda is burying the dead. You get your little butt back here. You hear me?"

"I hear you. Thank you, Jolene."

"You're welcome, Shining Sugah. Out."

I scrunched up my face. "How am I supposed to get home?"

"You'll have a long walk."

My face must have said that I was not amused.

Jagger chuckled, a sound that traveled along my skin and bones and nerves like fire, to settle low in my belly. "I've been offered a bike with a sidecar," he said. "Amos will ride my bike. Cupcake will be provided one of my private bikes. We'll have a small escort for protection, insisted upon by Whip and McQuestion, and they'll be driving your ATVs."

So they would know exactly where the junkyard was. I could refuse the escort, or dismiss them before we got there, but that wouldn't last long. I focused on the other crap in his statements. "Sidecar?" I growled. "I hate sidecars." My mother had died in one, but I didn't say that. Instead I shot him an *I will hurt you when I am well* look.

Jagger just grinned. "And when we get home, we'll revisit that expression."

"Home?"

"McQuestion has offered to give the junkyard provisional chapter house status."

My eyes might have bugged out of my head. "You could have led with that, Asshole." I shoved my good arm under me to sit up.

"Whip says you can ride with his personal house if you'd rather. Same invitation from both Bengal and Mama-Killer. Marconi offered to adopt you as family. I thought the clubs might go to war right then." Asshole seemed to find imminent war among biker clubs amusing. He adjusted the med-bay mattress so I could relax.

As the mattress moved to better support me, all kinds of thoughts meandered through my head, the kind that I'd have to look at later, after I was no longer druggy. Family beckoned, though I'd probably have to kill Mina if I went with Marconi. And I'd have to turn Whip into a thrall to keep him from getting shot if I went that route.

My own chapter house in the OMW though. *That* had possibilities.

"Thanks," I said, as the bed stopped moving and pain from being shifted eased.

Not looking at me, Jagger said oh so nonchalantly, "To keep bloodshed from happening, Cupcake suggested the junkyard become neutral territory."

I blinked. "Neutral . . ." Goose bumps rose on my flesh. "What did you say?" I willed him to look at me, but he didn't meet my eyes. "Jagger. Neutral territory?"

"Your own MC."

"My own motorcycle club . . . ?"

"Yeah. Something like a road house or central clearing house or trading post, autonomous and self-supporting, dealing equally with all the clubs and all of them having access to you. All that's on the table. All of it. You get to decide your fate, which is about as good as it gets, Little Girl."

"But how? People die when they walk away from a club."

"Not always. McQuestion and the prez would have to release you. You'd turn in your kutte. Design your own colors and insignia, your own emblems, draw up your own charter." He shrugged slightly, still not looking at me. "You'd be president. You'd have to assign a VP, treasurer, sergeant-at-arms. Pick your own enforcers, top guns."

"Bloooody buggering damn," I whispered. I wasn't joining another club. But. My own chapter house or neutral territory. Yeah. One of those. I could be a trading hub, pass-through hub, supply warehouse, a place for negotiations and drinking, I could have a roadhouse, even housing. Guns checked at the gate and no fighting allowed. And I could ban anyone for life if my rules were broken. *My* rules. Cupcake could be my chief negotiator. I could make money. I could . . .

Turn in my old kutte.

The cold turned into a shiver. I'd not be OMW anymore, and I was OMW to the core.

Except that . . . Yeah.

Pops had foreseen this possibility. It's why he'd sent me this direction, giving me the junkyard in his will, his best gift among the papers delivered to me after his death.

When Jagger spoke again, his tone was different. More stilted, laced with a forced casualness. "And. Uh." He moved a little to the side so his face was turned away slightly. "Because of that proposed status change, McQuestion released me from service and gave me club retirement."

I blinked again. "People don't retire from OMW."

"It was added to the charter at the end of the war. Members who survived major battles with honor are offered retirement. Such as it is."

"Meaning it's not fishing at the beach or moving to Hawaii so much as gaining a little more freedom?"

"A lot more freedom, but yeah. More or less. I was offered retirement after the Battle of Mobile. Turned it down. I took it this time." His mouth quirked down fast before he controlled whatever that reaction had been. "And then McQuestion told me that my job would be to get the new, temporary chapter house—or whatever you put together—up to standards." His eyes flicked to me and away. His mouth relaxed and turned up in a small smile. "And locate and catalogue your supplies, especially the military gear. He seemed to think my retirement would best be used as your enforcer."

"You know I'm not showing you my stuff."

For some reason that made Jagger happy. "I waited until he signed the papers retiring me before I told him he'd made a mistake. He should have just released me provisionally from being his top enforcer, not released me from active duty. When the papers were signed, I reminded McQuestion about a few other clauses in national club laws authorized after the Battle of Mobile. Once I'm retired, I'm my own man. McQuestion can't have it both ways, and returning to an active role in the club is up to me, not him." Jagger tilted his head back and forth as if considering and added, "Barring us all going to war again."

"And?"

"And he tried to tear up the papers. I told him to go fuck himself."

Bloody hell. "And how did all that go over?"

"He was pissed. Bashed in the teeth of his own new enforcer for not telling him that. Big Dick McKraken wanted my job and didn't offer the correct advice. Big Dick now has very few front teeth, and Oil Man Durbage now has my old job." Jagger seemed to find all that amusing.

"Once the other club leaders heard about my position change, people started bashing heads. Couple people got shot before things calmed down again."

"Wish I'd been a fly on that wall."

"I got the vid for later. Maybe one night after some more hot sweaty sex we can watch movies in bed."

I suddenly felt all better. "Popcorn and movies sounds nice, but McQuestion screwed up twice: letting you have retirement and giving up the junkyard."

His brown eyes finally turned to me, waiting, something amused and tender in their depths.

"You're free. And no matter which option I choose, Smith's won't be just a junkyard anymore." The clubs were boxing me in, caging me. But they also wanted me. It had been a long time since I had been wanted for *me*, and for the service I provided. It had been a long time since I felt a case of the warm fuzzies. This odd feeling might be that sensation.

And Jagger. Free. Wanting me.

I needed to study the OMW laws amended after the Battle of Mobile. I wondered if Jolene had a lawyer mode.

Spy took that moment to jump up onto the med-bay and step into my lap. She curled into a ball and started purring. Maul followed, still stiff and moving gingerly, but healing. He curled up at my side and yawned. It seemed my warm fuzzies included cats. I let my injured hand slide to Spy's head and said, "Thank you." I looked at Jagger and repeated the thanks.

"Don't thank me yet. The clubs don't know about Mateo planning to bomb the bunker."

My face must have done something, because he smiled slightly. "Yeah. They may shoot you when you tell them that. Or go to war over you. Or stab each other in the back over you. Which may account for the attack at the junkyard. So we should take precautions on the way home."

"Son of a bitch. The clubs are gonna ambush us, aren't they?"

"Some might. Most likely. But we'll get home."

My heart warmed at his use of the word *home*. As if he meant it for real, and not because he was a thrall.

"And I have to say, Little Girl, being with you won't be boring."

About the Author

Faith Hunter is a New York Times and USA Today best-selling author. She writes dark urban fantasy, paranormal urban thrillers, paranormal police procedurals, and science fiction.

Her long-running, bestselling, Skinwalker series features Jane Yellowrock, a hunter of rogue-vampires. The Soulwood series features Nell Nicholson Ingram in paranormal crime solving novels. Her Rogue Mage novels, a dark, post-apocalyptic fantasy series, features Thorn St. Croix, a stone mage in an alternate reality. She also writes a Scifi novella series: Junkyard Cats.

Under the pen name Gwen Hunter, she has writ-ten action adventure, mysteries, thrillers, women's fiction, a medical thriller series, and even historical religious fiction. As Gwen, she was part of the WH Smith Literary Award for Fresh Talent in the UK, and won a Romantic Times Reviewers Choice Award in 2008. Under all her pen names, she has over 40 books in print in 30 countries. Faith has won numerous awards and *Curse on the Land* won an Audie Award for 2017.

In real life, Faith once broke a stove by refusing to turn it on for so long that its parts froze and the un-used stove had to be replaced. She collects orchids and animal skulls, rocks and fossils, loves to sit on the screened back porch in lightning storms, and is a workaholic with a passion for whitewater kayaking and RV travel. She prefers Class III whitewater rivers with no gorge to climb out of, and drinks a lot of tea.

Some days she's a lady. Some days she ain't.

www.faithhunter.net   www.gwenhunter.com
www.facebook.com/official.faith.hunter